God is Blue
and other short stories

God is Blue
and other short stories

Gerry Pratt

Timber Press   Forest Grove, Oregon

Cover design: Patti Miller

Back cover photo: Patty Williams

ISBN: 0-917304-38-1
Library of Congress Catalog Card Number: 78-13889

Printed in the United States of America.

Timber Press
P.O. Box 92
Forest Grove, OR 97116

Introduction

The truth of life is revealed to each one of us one day at a time. I can remember Momma spitting on my burnt finger to take away the pain and saying, "that will teach you about fooling with matches." She had other lessons like, "you get back what you give out," and "don't ask man, but ask God in the midst of you." That one she learned at a revival.

Our living lessons come like that, a mixture of pain and laughter, but recorded for a lifetime in the quiet voice of the soul. These are the recordings of some of the days and some lessons spoken by mine.

Contents

God is Blue

God is blue. I had always thought God was white and then once as a child I saw a movie, *Cabin in the Sky*, in which Rochester was having an affair with Lena Horne when God interposed. He was black.

There was some problem about accepting God as black. It wasn't because of any appreciable prejudice but because whether in alabaster, on Sunday School cards, or appearing in Christian calendars, God was always white, except that day when He came to the Jews as a burning bush.

Later some forest loving naturalist started the story that "God is green" and put it on bumper stickers and scrawled it on woody trails. And whenever I went into the woods, or lay in the grass of springtime, I was easily convinced He was, indeed, green.

But sometimes, in the mid-summer harvest of the berry patch, there comes a moment that becomes a day, that becomes two or three, when God is blue.

To truly accept the blue you must begin in the days when we collected the lard tins from the bakery behind our house on Third Avenue West. They were tall, brass-finished cans with wire handles on the sides. By summer we usually had five or six of them.

In the mornings, they would be filled with sandwiches of peanut butter and jam and a cool jar of water. We would each carry one onto the interurban car that ran to Lullu Island where the peat bogs spread forever.

There are ticky-tack houses now across the breadth of Lullu Island and it no longer spreads forever. It spreads to Marpole and New Westminster and the Fraser River and seems quite small cut up into the black strips of pavement and stamp-size lawns. Contractors with machines have scraped off the five feet of peat bog and poured foundations for that progress.

But back then the peat bog was waist high to a tall man in berry bush and beneath the leaves that rustled in the Island wind grew the small, tart blueberries, wild and free for the picking.

"Plunk." The first echoing of the first berry striking the bottom of the five gallon lard can was the beginning of what seemed the impossible challenge. "Plunk. Plunk." And after a time as the sun rose and you climbed deeper under the brush to escape, the bottom was covered and by lunch you should be half way there.

Eileen picked beside me and sometimes in the afternoon, she would tip her can into mine like a good sister should.

"There. Now you don't have so much to go." And, primed with her berries, I would pick faster for awhile.

We cradled the cans carefully on the ride home. To shake them "took them down" and if they settled, they didn't look so full.

It wasn't until they stood, cans belly to belly on the kitchen table in the evening, the soft faint smell of the fresh berries large in the room, that you began to know what you had. Cooked with a touch of sugar, they were preserved in quart jars for winter with enough left fresh for the blueberry pies come Sunday.

Now, in the lady's field across the street where I am invited sometimes to come and help myself to the large, cultivated, juicy ripe blueberries, I wonder how quickly I could fill a lard can there. My children don't come. They are busy they say. And that's too bad, because in a summer field, low beneath the leaves, you can find God. And He's blue.

Bathtub Ring

It is a long time now since I have seen a Saturday night bathtub ring, the kind of ring painted with knee scrapings from a day at marbles in the dirt, mixed with a strong base of bicycle chain oil and a good sprinkling of baseball diamond dust for body.

Yet there it was, smudged and set to cool against the gleaming white enamel face of the tub just as if it had been jelled from the penetrating soap suds of forty years ago. And in an instant, I could see again the steam rise from the old four-legged tub, clouding the mirror and laying the curls of Momma's auburn hair flat against her forehead.

"Close the door. Close the door. You will let the steam out." Already a sudden cloud had escaped the room and the chill from the upstairs landing touched the buttocks of the four or five of us lined up with towels and apprehensive eyes.

"It's too hot. Too hot. Ouch." You could hear the hollering clear to the kitchen, they said, as one by one we slipped, gently, oh, ever so gently, down the sloping end of the tub into the hot water. It turned you scarlet and then pink in a line where the water rose against your skin and was so hot you were afraid to move.

Momma attacked like she attacked the Irish Fiddle on wash day, Fels Naptha bar in one hand, a hard, skin scraping sponge in the other, down your back, then scooping the water so that it cascaded over your head and hair, carrying the eye searing soap suds over your face so that you didn't dare holler or move. For a minute, it was pure hell, the scrubbing in kettle-hot water, the soap suds seeping into your tightly shut eyes, your legs, and hollerings filling the tub.

And then you were done. Oh, the warm, clear water that took away the suds, the hot towel to wipe your eyes and suddenly it was a gentle world, soft and pink, and Momma catching her breath was resting on the closed toilet seat admiring her work. "I'd never know you were the same kids," she used to say. "I thought you were somebody else's until I got the dirt off you."

Then she would let us "soak," she said, while she brushed the hair from her eyes and went downstairs to get our night shirts from the warming oven above the kitchen stove.

When it came time to get out the room had begun to chill, yet we delayed as long as we could, squirting the soap beneath the suds and splashing so that the floor was an inch in water it seemed. One at a time Momma wrapped us in the towels, rubbing hard to bring the pink to a higher tone, and then chased us off to bed. It was that picture of the draining tub, the murky water in the end, rattling and sucking down the drain once she had pulled the plug, that stayed in your mind. There, in mute testimony that we were indeed clean, was the Saturday night ring that had been lifted from our hides.

It always felt as if we had left something of ourselves behind, something that had disappeared with the bathwater on those nights. In time we grew so that the girls were too big to bathe with the boys all in one tub at one time and it was true, something of us had left with the suds.

And now, as stepping out onto this precise, clean bathroom floor, the overhead fan constantly clearing away the steam, it is with a start that you see that ring around the tub. The mixture is different, dirt from the leaves, maybe a little lawnmower grease, and some from the barn where we had been moving hay to make room for storage. Not such a far cry from real boy dirt. For a minute, just that minute it takes for the picture to rise again from

4

the backroads of your mind, it reminds you of those Saturday night baths and how precious they were in helping a body stay clean.

Momma's Own Brand of Exorcism

Suddenly, everybody is up with the exorcist or exorcism. I can't help laughing because there is this movie review on the television and people are being interviewed after they have seen the movie about exorcism.

"I fainted, I actually fainted," says one girl. And my kid watching the television swears softly: "I gotta see that movie."

"I couldn't stand it," says a young fellow next out of the theater. "The noises, the vomiting, almost made me sick. I had to get out of there." And my kid mutters again, "I gotta see that movie."

"It's only for adults," says my kid's mother as more people are coming out telling what a gruesome thing it is they have put on film. And I gotta laugh some more.

Listen. I know what they are talking about, it being terrible and all. I've known about this exorcism since I was a kid. What's more, I am thinking, what with things like they are today, maybe I should go back to practicing a little exorcism on my own.

The world we came through in the '30s was full of exorcism.

That's nothing to do with the Father Divine hallelujah meetings or old Mrs. Osbourne whom Momma called in once to sit on the edge of my brother's bed because he was seeing white lights in the night. That kind of exorcism was gentle by comparison with the potent stuff. The real exorcism, which the dictionary says quite properly is the "driving out of evil spirits by ritual or incantation," was something else.

You gotta remember this was the day of the string tied around your aching tooth and fastened to the door knob. Come to think of it, the hundred or more times I know we tried that I never did see a tooth come out on the string, even the loose ones. These were also the days when you didn't have a thermometer to stick into everyone's "whatever" the moment they felt sick to the stomach or grew flush in the face.

But those were the days of wet feet and winter colds and probably more bedroom cases of pneumonia than anyone will ever know. And if Momma wasn't the greatest exorcist the world has ever seen, then you gotta show me.

It began with the sniffles. "Stop that sniffling or blow your nose," was Momma's opening challenge. And you knew that if you didn't stop the sniffling, exorcism was just ahead. Momma watched from the moment of the first running nose. She would put a hand on your face for your temperature and look menacingly into your ideas. "You're not coming down with anything. Get on with you."

The next day a cough, flush face. You tried hard to hide it. First up in the morning. Act cheerful. Get the wood for the woodbox. Maybe she won't notice. "Come here. Open your mouth. How do you feel?" No matter what you said, Momma usually had it figured by the second day and you were not going outside, even if it was Saturday.

Then it began. If it was a cough, the very worst thing in Momma's mind, it was a mustard plaster on brown paper. God will only testify as to how she did it, but the whole black pepper and mustard mess was slapped onto the bare skin of your chest like a cold wet rag. Then it began to burn. Sometimes, if she was really exorcising, she would wrap the plaster in a strip of sheeting to hold in the heat and you could feel the devil being burned right through your rib cage.

It was a ritual, all right, complete with incantation. Momma made it so miserable nobody would dare to get a cold. If they did, there wasn't a moment to lose in getting rid of it.

If the germ was loose in the house, everyone had to be protected. If the season was right, it would begin with a great kettle of leeks set to boiling on the stove all day long. Leeks are those green onions with white bulbs on the bottom about as sweet as daffodil roots, and when they are stewed like that, they stink in your skin for a week. Sometimes, when she was really fighting the devil cold, you would get leeks around your neck for awhile—just in the house, of course. People, even in those days, would think Momma was crazy for believing an onion could do a cold any good.

Then there was eucalyptus. Most of you think eucalyptus is a tree that shelters the Australian bushwacker, eh? Well, Momma's eucalyptus came in a brown bottle and she put it on a spoon and held your nose while she offered the incantation, "Open your mouth, this'll do you good." It tasted so bad, even with a spoonful of sugar right behind, that the words "Open your mouth," had a Pavlov's dog effect that set you to retching. "None of that now ," Momma would say. "That costs money, you just swallow it down. We didn't ask for this cold in this house."

There were other things in Momma's exorcism. Good things like dandelion wine, fresh from the crock by the stove or off the preserve shelf in the basement—wine that burned in your tummy and made the older kids laugh when they were given a glassful for spring. And she believed in honey and lemon juice, when there were lemons to be had. That helped undo the evils of wet feet and damp clothes.

And when it was all done and she had given you the leeks and the mustard plasters and the eucalyptus on a spoon, Momma would come and sit on the side of your bed at the end of the day and gently rock the springs. I can remember sleeping and waking late into the night to the gentle rocking of the bed. She was there in the dark, chasing the devil and his sickness out of her kids with the only kind of exorcism she knew. Only then we called it prayer and we are alive, all ten of us, to this day.

The movie? I tell the kids, "You want to see that movie? Wait until you catch yourself a cold and I'll take you to Gram's house and I'll show you an exorcist that puts them all to shame."

True Warmth

It is cold and I don't like it. The furnace went off and my feet are cold and even with my hands in my pants pockets, I can feel the cold in my fingers. It reminds me of things I don't want to remember. But I will.

Cold. So cold that the frost from your sleeping breath has formed a fog of ice inside the bedroom window. Scrape at it with your fingers and small piles of crushed ice roll up under your nails at the tips of your fingers. You breathe close against the glass and then rub your sleeve at the spot to clear a small circle to look outside. The sun is out, bright and orange on the leaves that lie naked and dead in small heaps where the wind has swept them against the fence.

Everything is cold. Your pants are cold when you pull them over your legs and your shoes and socks are cold so that your cold feet fit into them formally and impersonally.

The cold follows you down the stairs and into the kitchen where the stove is cold and there is more frost on the inside of the window glass.

The first thing is to take out the ashes, shake 'em loose from the grate and then carry the dead gray remains of yesterday's warmth across the floor, carefully so that only small and invisible sands of ash fall off the paper and onto the linoleum. You cannot see what has fallen, but it is there beneath your feet in a soft, chill, crunching path between the stove and the back door.

There is no warmth. The water runs chilled from the tap for the kettle and the paper and dry wood in the stove box sit still and unpromising.

The great headed Diamond match from the warming oven is like a wand. It holds the beginning of the goodness for the day. As you stroke it across the iron stove plate, it growls and in an exploding soft snarl, shoots a yellow-blue flame up the stick of the match so that the shaft turns black on the end as it curls in its own heat and flame. Now carry that magic to the paper and the kindling in the stove.

There is a response, a throaty pulling of the draught from the damper and the iron stove lids, set back into place, begin to reflect the combustion heat of the wood and the paper and the flames inside. Cold drops of tap water trail across the side of the steel kettle and explode, pummelling the hot stove lids. Then, curling your chilled finger into one another, you press your hands together above the stove and welcome the warm.

The porridge kettle filled with soaking oatmeal, water and salt is pulled forward and in time begins the gentle bubbling that brings a crust to the mush and fills the room with its own live scent of life and strength.

To bring from that long cold night those first warm moments of day, is to bring life into winter. From the first moment of laying a naked foot pad onto the floor and slipping your rump from beneath the blankets, it is a matter of will and determination; you wait rather than go to the toilet while the day is yet so cold; you don't even splash water to your face until there is the promise of warmth. And then, at the kitchen sink, in one last challenge to the winter, you splash the tap water into your face, exploding the breath from between your lips and hand cup the water again and again to your skin, to your ears. Good God, you are awake and alive.

Only on days such as this, when the furnace mechanism fails and the automatic thermostat dead sticks your demand to awaken the heat, only then do you remember those other days of winter. There is no such challenge in the insulated, gas furnaced house with the thick bedroom carpets. Winter wakes you now with an alarm clock and waits patiently for a nip at your ears in the dash between the house and the car. And the days of winter now are gentle and without determination.

But cold, good cold in the morning that says you must warm yourself to begin, that is an inspiration. "Damn, it's cold. This is ridiculous the furnace not working." And your curses for the broken apparatus and your stamping and arm waving are only for show. In truth, it is good to know that warmth, true warmth begins from inside and it's there yet when called.

Dandelion Wine

If we had aged the dandelion wine, it would be close to forty years old today. It was the color of brandy wine, amber, and stood still and potent in the glass when poured carefully so that none of the silt was stirred up from the bottom of the bottle. The taste was aromatic, like a sharp sherry or very strong German wine, but aside from that, it had a taste of its own.

If you have never been a cheap wine drinker, it would be difficult to understand how the Skid Road people come up with names like "Sneaky Pete" for some particular $1.29 bottle of poison. But wine can be like that, soft and warm to taste, harmless and friendly going down until suddenly it has stolen away your sanity and you are left in a euphoria of loose lipped, foot stumbling, finger fumbling relaxation. Dandelion wine was the worst.

Our dandelion wine began high on the Plains of Abraham above Spanish Banks by the sea where the yellow-headed dandelions covered the fields in a sea of gold blossoms through the first wet, warm days of spring. We would pluck the heads between our fingers until the pollen dusted deep into the skin.

It was a stoop harvest, much like the row crop workings of the migrants today, only it lacked the urgency of picking for food and sustenance. We felt like amateur moonshiners. Winemaking, even dandelion winemaking, was against the moral principles of our neighbors in the block. And when we stuffed the heads into a sugar sack and set them to soaking in the crock behind the stove, Momma would hide the whole thing under a blanket if there was an outsider coming to call.

Yet, hide it you couldn't. The smell of the pungent dandelions working with raisins and sugar all but thundered through the house. It worked into our clothes and became a part of the taste of everything we ate for a time.

And when the brewing was done and the bottles filled, funnel and ladle measuring out the ambrosia, we pushed in the corks or screwed on the bottle tops and laid the thirty or more bottles of the batch across the shelves of the preserves cupboard in the basement. Oh, there would be tastes during the brewing, a spoonful to see if it was working, a small glass if it happened to be a cold day or a moment when someone needed a lift. Dandelion wine could do wonders for you even while it was young and in the crock.

But the real days of expectation came after the bottles had been laid away in the quiet and darkness of the basement beyond the woodpiles. They were as secure and safe there as they would have been in an ammunition dump. Because to stand near the new wine was to stand in a dangerous place.

Regularly, in the midst of dinner or in the quiet of the night or even through the noise of a family shouting match there would come the musket shot blast of a bursting wine bottle. But by October's day, it was safe again and from day to day the magic medicine of the dandelion would be administered for physical and emotional ills, providing health and happiness at winter's darkest moments.

The brew's final days were always in spring, usually about the middle of March. By that time our potion had been "aged," as we knew it, and the alcohol had grown robust and the wine kicked some as it passed over the tongue. It was then Momma went to the last bottles and poured the water glass to the brim: "Take this. It's springtime and you need it," she would say, and we would line up with the magic of booze in our eyes, the girls pinching their noses to swallow it down. Only when she discovered my brothers sipping and savoring, did Momma begin to get apprehensive about the curative effects and begin to take notice of the loud voices and sudden outbursts of laughter that followed the wine.

But it was a tonic, marvelous to behold. And if we had held it longer, I'd take a glass today.

A Visit to the Barber

On the late television commercials you can sometimes see them selling those do-it-yourself hair cutting kits. Poppa is in the chair and his wife is zipping this thing up his neck just like it's induction day all over again. As his ears begin standing free and his wife is smiling into the cameras, a pitch man begins explaining how you can make enough money for a vacation trip to Europe just by cutting your own hair.

He's not kidding. The price of haircuts has been going up faster than Arab bank balances. I am of this century, and I can remember haircuts at two bits a clip, and I can remember barbers who thought a razor cut was something you tried to patch over with toilet paper.

No more. Even that old saw—"Shave and a haircut, six bits" seems to have been something out of the 18th Century. I mean, haircuts today are four dollars apiece, with an appointment, and if you don't leave the barber a half or more, chances are you are a long time between appointments. Some guys are even turning to beauty parlors where it is a matter of hair styling and you never know what that's going to cost.

Why so agitated? Well, it's great to have the barber make a buck. But it has just been suggested to my heir apparent that he see about getting his biblical hairstyle shortened to conform with the job market. This kid says he would, but he can't afford it. The only kids who are getting haircuts these days are the ones going through the recruiting centers. The haircut is one of today's military fringe benefits that has real meaning.

What we need in this era of nostalgia is a return to the real barbershop, like the one we had on Yew Street in a store front. The barber there was a World War II Irish Fuselier who learned his trade in His Majesty's Service. He was gray in the face and brutal with the clippers when I knew him, tired around the shoulders, his arms dropping to his sides, he would let out a burst of air with every series of passes at your head. It was exhausting work, and looking back you can see now that his feet must have resented the job terribly. You could tell by the way he laid down his newspaper and looked up when you came through the door. There was a small bell over the door in case he was in the toilet in the back of the shop and he was there a lot in the late years when he cut hair with a glassy-eyed stare and made wild, reckless passes with the clippers.

Those were not the electric clippers you kids know about today. They were squeeze clippers and this old barber would hook his arthritic fingers around the handles and squeeze, clip, clip. Sometimes, when he was tired, he would pull the clippers away half way through the squeeze and the hair would come out by the roots. "Oops. Gotcha that time," and he would wipe the back of his hand across his nose in a gesture of apology.

There was a smell about the barbershop in those days, whisky maybe. Or it could have been the hard hair tonic the barber used to rub into the bristles he left standing across the top of your skull. That was a strange, powerful tonic, mostly water, but enough of some secret military potion mixed in to make it sit up like cement. When the barber combed your hair, the bristles popped up on each side above the ears, and the part looked like it had been sliced in stone. Neither wind nor rain would ease that line for a week or more.

"Good morning," said the barber, as if it was really your idea and he was not too committed to it at all. He tucked the paper into the back of his chair and pushed himself to his feet. There was pain in the way he would reach for the soiled sheet that hung over the back of the barber chair.

"Shave. Or just a haircut?" He would laugh at that and pinch your cheeks between his fingers. "No. That's just bum fuzz lad. But wait awhile; shaving is a blessing that comes later."

And he would slap the board across the arms of the barber chair and stand back while you climbed into the perch. It was then you handed him the quarter. With that he began, starting low on the nape of your neck beneath the line where the sheet tucked into your shirt so that the small clippings dropped down your back and drew your shoulder blades into a tense twitch.

"Easy now. Sit still. That pull a little? Well, sit still or we are going to lose an ear."

There was no question about style. You got into the chair and he turned you away from the mirror and left you facing the door until he was finished, right to the point where he whipped the lather from his shaving mug and scraped the straight razor down your neck. "Clean at the back the way your mother wants it," he would say.

Then with a flourish he would spin the chair, whip away the sheet so the hair clippings flew up into your face and ask with sudden authority in his voice, "That's better, eh?"

And for an instant, summer or winter, you would look into the face of a stranger, a thin boy with oh, such large and protruding ears. And then the barber would thumb press to your head those hairs that stood up in defiance of his secret tonic and push you out of the chair. Outside the air struck cool and fresh to the naked sides of your head.

You took the haircut home so Momma could see if you got your money's worth. She always seemed a little hurt when you came home from the barbershop. It was as if you had grown a little while you had been away. After she looked it over and told you it looked nice, you knew somewhere inside that indeed you had. And all for a quarter.

Angelo Pappas

In the wonderful world of Angelo Pappas everything was possible. Angelo looked out at the world through great brown eyes, brown eyes that looked purple they were so deep and mellow.

Angelo was the best green apple thief in town. Old Man Mason would pick up a stick at the very sight of Angelo coming, innocent and nonchalant, down the alley beneath Mason's transparent tree. And sometimes Angelo didn't even feel like an apple. But Old Man Mason never took chances.

Angelo's old man ran the fruit stand in the railroad station. Angelo worked there on Saturdays and stole a dime now and then from the cash drawer, or some fruit to eat at home. Other times he would sit in Mrs. Evans' den and read the National Geographic Magazine while the rest of us made noises playing cowboys or bandits and cops in the sawdust by the furnace in the basement.

It didn't matter whether Angelo was stealing apples or reading the National Geographic, we all understood he was getting ready for something. All his life we knew Angelo was getting ready. And then in spring, about this time it was, he told us.

Angelo didn't make any big deal of what he was doing, what he had been getting ready for. He just started doing it and the first thing he did was come into Third Avenue West with an empty coffee can on the first hot sunshine day and begin prying up the soft tar from the pavement. He did that for a long time. Whenever it was hot enough for the sun to soften the tar, Angelo was in the street prying it up into his coffee can.

And then he got boards and cleared a place in the Pappas' backyard and began the work and we could see what it was he was doing. Angelo was building a ship.

It was not a great ship, but big enough to do anything that could be conceived in the mind of a twelve-year-old. It was indeed a miracle because of the tools. He had a hammer that was used to break open the banana crates at his poppa's fruit stand, a saw, a kitchen knife and the boards that were taken from where Mernie Sommer's dad was building a duplex on Fourth Avenue.

Angelo put the boards together in a point at one end and nailed a seat across the middle and a stern board or two to hold it together at the back. By late July, maybe we were into August, he began pressing the tar into the cracks between the boards.

Now the world had never heard of Onassis or Nicharios in those days. The Greek shipping magnates just didn't exist. But whatever it was that created them was at work in Angelo that spring he built his ship.

When it was summer quiet and the world slowed around our games of kick-the-can or smoking leaves wrapped in toilet paper or fishing off Fraser's wharf, we would visit Angelo at his ship. He would sit there in the grass by the boat, the tar stuck black to his fingers, smiling from somewhere in the world behind those tender eyes and say, "Sure we can sail to Bowen Island. Just wait."

He didn't have a sail yet, but that would come. "We got to test her first," he explained. And Angelo held up the paddles he had cut from extra boards. "These will get us there and back. Then when we get to know her, we can go any place, any place there's water."

Angelo and his brothers Johnny Pappas and Billy, the little Pappas and me and some other guys helped carry the boat to the foot of Trutch Street where the water came in deep by the rocks.

Maybe something happened when we dropped it once or twice, maybe that loosened up something. Still the boat looked fine there on the beach with Angelo's paddles shipped aboard and the thick streaks of tar running between the cracks where the boards came together.

What happened then was so wet and so quick it is impossible to recall the sequence, only that there was Angelo in the boat and the boat was going down, very fast. And there was Angelo with the paddles floating beside his head, and Angelo with all his clothes on kicking and struggling toward the beach.

We sat there with him an hour waiting for the boat to surface again. "It was wood," Angelo said, "and it will float." But only the paddles came back and finally we walked home, Angelo's wet trousers whispering between his legs.

The last I saw of Angelo Pappas was long after he moved. He was in a blue sailor's uniform and shipping to a base in England. We stood on the street corner and tried to remember the names of all the kids that used to steal Old Man Mason's apples. And Angelo he said to me, "Those were good times. We had good times then didn't we?" And I'm wondering now if he even remembered the ship he built and if what we think we are getting ready for in life has anything to do with what life has in mind for us.

Karnile Sing

Karnile Sing drove a large, red Ford wood truck. I know it was a Ford because the Ford V-8 engines and the Ford transmissions and the Ford body work gave off a special Ford sound in those days. Any kid who knew anything about cars could tell you what a Ford sounded like.

Karnile showed up with his first red wood truck when we were in the sixth grade. He quit coming to school and drove up one day in that truck loaded with Hindus. It was like a Jewish boy being Bar Mitzvah when a Hindu in our neighborhood got his first wood truck.

It was obvious no one had taught Karnile to drive. He crashed and ground the gears with a determination that was matched only by the big truck's steel and stamina. They both survived.

You gotta picture Karnile Sing to capture the scene. He chewed some kind of wooden stick instead of brushing his teeth. He tried to teach me to use it but it ripped into all my cavities. The stick made his teeth movie-star bright and white. He was tanned like a Malibu sun freak, golden skinned you could call it, with waves of slick 'em shiny hair that tossed in carefree curls across his forehead. He wore a white shirt open to the navel, enough to send any starlet overboard.

And there he was, overnight, the local wood man. We had seen the Hindus for years prowling the alleyways with their wood trucks. "You wanna buy a good load of wood? Five dollars. All fir slabs. Not wet. Dry load." The sales pitch was intended to establish the price and to identify the wood. "All fir" usually meant the slabs, trimmed from the lumber mill logs, were fir on top of the load and maybe cedar, not nearly so slow burning, and hemlock beneath. The testimony to the dryness of the load was necessary because most of the mills cut logs that had been rafted from Northern Vancouver Island and the salt water took months, even warm basement wood piles, to dry out enough to burn. In winter, wet wood was a catastrophe.

The wood men were mostly older with graying beards and black turbans wrapped around their heads. The only time you would see them out of their wood trucks is when they would appear at the drugstore on Burrard Street with all the little Hindu kids, girls in ankle long dresses and earrings, even though they were only four and five years old, the boys, running noses, hand wiped incessantly on a knuckle or a sleeve, all hollering Hindu for the old man to buy 'em an ice cream. And he usually did.

But Karnile was different. He read things, he even enjoyed Kipling, though he used to swear to me that the stories were not true, that the white man in India wasn't nearly such a hero. Karnile knew that because he had uncles who came from India and they told him things that made him angry about the Queen being Empress of India, Star of the East and so on. That was before we knew what race was and believed the British Empire was a thing forever, even in Canada we thought that.

Karnile liked my sister and he walked home with her a few times and he talked about going to the University and about going back to India someday. If you were going to write a Hindu version of "How Green Was My Valley," you would come up with a character like Karnile. He was going to be a doctor one day, lawyer the next and the political leader of his people at other times, all shaped in the vision of our sixth grade world, though Karnile was a little old for the sixth, maybe twelve or thirteen when the rest of us were eleven.

He never said anything about the wood business. Chewing that stick of his, he would clap his hands together to show you how fast and certain he would change the world. "Yes sir, when it's my turn, Hindus will be teachers, we are the best teachers you know. Yes sir, Karnile Sing, your Hindu doctor. You wait and see." Yet there he was one day, grinning from ear to ear like they had given him a lobotomy and changed everything. He was hootin' and hollering about the truck and loading it up with Hindu kids like he had just liberated the Punjab.

I watched him from the curb, trying to remember my friend. We were going to join the Socialist Party together when we were old enough and there he was swathed in the aroma of fresh wet sawdust acting like nothing else mattered but the big red Ford. In time, a very short time, he began to wear a turban himself and I would see him prowling the lanes in the bruised and fender torn Ford hawking over the fences to peddle the fir slabs. Once I stopped him and climbed on the running board. The truck seat was strewn with orange peelings and the floor of the Ford cab was worn through to the metal. Karnile smelled of sweat and only his teeth were as white and bright as I remembered. "What happened?" I asked. "Why are you doing this instead of going to school?"

He grinned at me, the boyish, careless wrinkles coming to his eyes. "Make money," he said. "You make lotsa money in the wood business." And he showed the money he had in his pocket.

I felt left out, he was a wood man first, a Hindu second. My friend seemed lost forever.

"How about asking your Mom? She want a good dry load. Just five dollars. This is good dry wood, I promise. You know I wouldn't cheat you. We are friends. Right? Good fir load. Five dollars. Ask your Mom."

The Other Dog

Uncle Billy Hassel had escaped my mind for thirty years. In all probability I couldn't clearly focus, even in mind's eye, on what he really looked like, though he was a big man, heavy set at the middle with a touch of that Hemingway display of masculinity and insecurity. What there was of him has been walled up in my memory along with that dog, something like walking with a small stone in your shoe that slips to the toe where it doesn't hurt anymore, yet is there just the same.

But then we bought this new dog. And when we brought the new dog home and opened a can of dog food, he ate it like a growing boy swallows a grape, and then spent the next fifteen minutes pushing the plate with his nose looking for more.

That triggered the memories. Still, it was not until the next day, in the morning, that Uncle Billy came into focus. The new dog wouldn't walk down the stairs and I had to pick it up, back strain and all, one hand beneath the hips, one under the chest, and carry it down. It was then, with each step, the dog in my arms smelling of fresh cedar shavings, that it all tumbled back into view.

We had owned a family dog once, a cocker named Ginger. At least Ginger is the name I remember the dog by, whether it came with that name or achieved it in joining our family, I was too young to determine. It was simply a name that signified a warm, gold, brown life in a cardboard box by the stove that one day ceased to be. There are traces of freshly spaded earth and the quiet mixture of remorse and love associated with the memory and Momma's firm admonition that became our cardinal rule always, "There will be no more dogs in this house."

It was sometime after that when Uncle Billy Hassel announced over his radio program the contest with the prize to be one of his champion collie dogs.

Uncle Billy's admission to our house was through the needle point speaker curtain on our cabinet sized Philco that stood in the corner of the living room on four, sow-like legs with a frowning face of knobs and an amber dial. My brother, who bought the radio secondhand, was fond of caressing the cabinet and telling us, "They don't make 'em like that anymore." He was right.

Billy Hassel is dead now so I can tell you with eased conscience that there were other programs we preferred to his, "Jack Armstrong, The All American Boy," or "Little Orphan Annie," were better. But even in those days Momma was concerned with our minds and she preferred Uncle Billy with his "Rig a Jig Jig and Away We Go..." or was it "Heigh Ho and Away We Go?" Whatever, it was better for our minds, what with all the guitar thrumming, loud singing and dog barking that Uncle Billy threw into the program. That dog of his carried on a one or two bark dialogue with Uncle Billy regularly, "Isn't that right Laddie?"

"Whoof Whoof." And if you had any imagination at all, you knew the dog understood every word.

"Now if you would like to own a dog just like Laddie, all of your own, then all you have to do is listen carefully." With that Uncle Billy dropped the bombshell. He would hold a contest to have kids sign up members for his radio club. The kid with the most new members would win the dog. "Right Laddie? Whoof Whoof." Indeed. We had four weeks to get the names and signatures. The first person to bring me out of the reverie of those possibilities was my sister. She had been listening from the doorway where she stood wiping the dinner dishes.

"Will you help me?" That was blurted out without a thought of Ginger or Momma's dictum.

"You don't have any wood in the woodbox," she said with sisterly authority. "That would make Momma happy if you kept the woodbox full."

"You heard him," I said. "That dog Uncle Billy is giving away. That's a valuable dog. People pay a lot for a collie like that." She looked dubious.

"I probably wouldn't win anyway."

"Why not?" she said and I knew she would help.

So there was Eileen and later Carl Luond from the bakery across the alley, the three of us traveling the school grounds at General Gordon and Bayview and Henry Hudson and St. Augustine's signing up kids for Uncle Billy Hassel.

We had maybe two or three thousand names on brown paper, wrapping paper, on personal stationery, names all wrapped up in fat bundles like lovers' memories. I took them down to the radio station myself.

"These are for Uncle Billy's radio club."

The receptionist looked up as if someone had walked across her lawn.

"They are my new members. For the contest."

She was looking at me but her mind was somewhere beyond that switchboard and for a minute there was no response. What she saw was a bad toothed smile in an over large head in need of a haircut all fastened to a boy in homemade short trousers with the flap-style fly open like a farm gate.

"Where did you get all that?" She was none too sure of the packet being pushed across her desk.

"My sister and some of my friends, but I got most of 'em myself." I wanted to ask who was winning the contest but suddenly I felt I had said too much already.

Two days later they announced I had won the collie dog. And when we got the dog home it was hungry. Momma, who had ten kids around the place at the time, didn't say anything.

"He should have about a pound of fresh meat a day, with mash," Uncle Billy Hassel had said, recommending several kinds of store bought mash that came in for more than the cost of our breakfast porridge. "Break it up so he eats twice a day at first," he said. So that first day I went with the dog to the butcher shop on Yew Street and they gave me big, bare knuckle bones that we cooked into dog soup. The next day the butcher wanted ten cents for bones.

The first night under the back porch we sat together, me holding the dog until she grew quiet, both of us watching the images of the backyard grow dim in the darkness, the broken apple tree, the sagging fence line. When she was still, I tied her leather strap to the porch post and went inside for dinner.

"Get washed. You have dog all over yourself." The tone of Momma's voice was enough to put you on your guard. But there was never a chance to wash. Instead, there was a wild scratching and whining at the back door. The dog had bitten her strap as if it had been cut with a razor. Only the short end hung loose from her neck.

I took her into the basement then and when the time was right we slipped upstairs to the bedroom, our movement screened by the evening British Empire musicals Momma played loudly on the Philco. The dog stayed flat across the foot of my bed all night and with the first light of day, I took her to the top of the stairs. She wouldn't move and began to whine when I threatened to leave her there.

In the end I carried her down and together we ran without stopping to the beach and played through the day in a pattern that made the days go swiftly. The dog ate a lot, there's nothing to deny about that. She ate the heel out of my brother's boot and my brother had only the one pair that fit. She ate the handle on the kitchen broom to a stub and chewed down the gladiolas Momma grew in the yard. But in between there were all the things a boy and a dog are made for, sticks flying into the ocean, the barking, gull chasing charges as she flew across the sand, ears flat, tongue flapping happily, the rolling, wrestling love of any boy for any dog.

It is hard to know, looking back, whether my mother spoke to Mr. Goodie the shoemaker or whether he got the idea himself. He had a son with the Royal Canadian Mounted Police. That day, in the lane behind his shop, the son was with him.

"Hey there Johnny." (He called all small boys by that name.)

"Hey." He stepped out into the lane determined to be heard. Mr. Goodie, with his carefully waxed mustache that tobacco had stained brown beneath the nostrils but curled gray to the pointed tips, was a friend. He allowed you to sit in the shop amid the smell of rubber cement and the humming of the lathe while he sanded down the new soles he nailed to old shoes.

The Mountie stepped into the lane behind him. He was dressed in the scarlet tunic that made him appear as if he belonged in a giant toy box. "Hi," he said and felt the dog, handling her with confidence that made the pup stretch and stand poised. "Want to sell her son?"

"No sir." The reply was almost a shout.

The Mountie looked quizzically at the shoemaker.

"Your Mom was down with one of your brother's boots, son, and she said the dog needed a good home. Yes she was. Kinda looking for you too, she was." In the long silence of that moment there were the images of an empty woodbox, the boot, the broom and the chewed gladiolas. His son was going north in the morning Mr. Goodie said. "He could make a policeman's dog outa her Johnny. You would like that."

Even now the only memory of what happened after that is of Mr. Goodie handing me a dollar bill. "Johnny, we have to make it legal. You take the dollar and buy something good for yourself." I knew then I couldn't change things. The Mountie had slipped a leather strap around the dog and held her close to his leg.

It was a long walk back up the lane toward home that day with Mr. Goodie's dollar bill in my hand and my dog barking in the shop behind.

I used to ask about the dog a lot, figuring that when she came back she would know me and I would know her. But Mr. Goodie told me one day that an Indian had shot her so I forgot about that dog and about Uncle Billy Hassel and about carrying her down the stairs in the morning smelling of fresh cedar shavings and her warm breath on my face.

Silk Pants

Jimmy Pennigar wasn't what you would call a fat little kid, but his cheeks were well filled and his short legs gave him the appearance of being on the cuddly side. He was one of seven or eight kids from the Pennigar family down the street. How many brothers or sisters you had was irrelevant in those days and the Pennigars were Catholic, too. It wasn't uncommon in families like the Pennigars for the old man to come home, look down the dinner table at the row of hungry faces and bellow at the top of his voice,

"OK. Now all the neighbor kids go on home." And nobody would leave.

There were several girls in his family with the same chubby cheek, dark haired genes that Jimmy carried. They were a little remote from the run-of-the-mill neighbor kids. Jimmy was too, for that matter, most of the time. But he could fight and damn, he could hit a baseball a country mile and he was usually the last out of the tree when Old Man Mason came thundering down the lane after the apple thieves ripping off his transparents in early summer.

We never paid too much special notice to Jimmy, him being quiet and all. But one day in early summer at Jericho Beach, when the bunch of us were skipping rocks and pushing boards out into the water and making rafts, suddenly, wet trousers, soaked shirts, it seemed warm enough to go swimming. We undressed behind the rushes in the dunes with everybody hollering and shoving and falling down in the sand in the rush to get naked and into the water, Jimmy took down his pants and he was wearing his sister's underwear.

They were silk panties, just like my sisters wore, only they were too big for Jimmy and they bagged all over the place like bloomers. He had his pants down to his knees before he remembered he had them on, I guess, and then it was too late. He just dropped his bare fanny into the sand and looked at us and waited. It was quiet for a minute, a thing like that took some time to adjust. There were those among us who didn't wear any underwear, didn't own any, and there were some who wore long johns handed down from their old man or a big brother. But silk pants?

"Hey, Pennigar. You got your old lady's drawers on?" Ernie Turner was the first to stand up and point.

The color was rising in Jimmy Pennigar's face.

The rest of us watched Ernie sifting sand through his fingers while he tried to figure the next move. Pennigar was down. It was just a matter of how to really put it to him, him pretending to be one of us and all.

"What you doing tonight, Sweet Jimmy?" Holland asked.

"You oughta try a brassiere," Ernie said. "They are really nice."

But none of the cracks got off the ground because Jimmy just sat there pouring sand out of his shoe and swatting at the sand fleas on his legs until he pulled his trousers back on.

We went swimming that day and Jimmy stood on the beach watching. He walked home with us too, quietly and off to one side where no one spoke to him. And after that he changed a lot. In pickup baseball games it usually went—"I pick Forbes, I pick Holland, I pick Turner, I pick Pratt," until the last man on the curb was Jimmy Pennigar. Even when we were short a man there were days Jimmy was left there when we took the field. He acted like he didn't care and got sarcastic when you talked to him and that made it worse. None of us ever tired of telling the new kids how Jimmy wore his sister's underpants. "Keep your eye on Pennigar, he wears silky underwear."

We lost track of Jimmy after awhile. He opened a florist shop somewhere in the suburbs and I remember him during the war with a collection of small dogs walking the beach or waiting it out on a park bench. But that's not the way he really wanted to grow up, him being able to hit a baseball the way he did. People have certain rights today. Jimmy had the right even then to wear silk pants if he wanted. I wish we had known that. He was really too good a hitter to lose.

Strawberry Fields

Oh, the strawberries are in the fields. They are so big and ripe and red and I love 'em. Why do I hate to pick them so?

I have. Who around this part of the country hasn't? I mean even before you "earned" an allowance you were picking berries. Used to be, and not so long ago, a great day in the strawberry field was worth a buck and a quarter, maybe a buck and a half if you didn't eat too many, didn't stop to talk and stuffed a bread and jam sandwich into your mouth as you worked without taking time out to eat.

Now? Now they make fifteen, maybe twenty dollars a day and the picking is easier too. Bigger bushes, just drive out and look and you will see. Those strawberry bushes now grow knee high to a middle-sized boy, and with bigger berries. Some of this year's crop look like winter apples.

That wasn't always the case. Strawberries once grew on straggly bushes and came thin and sun baked on runners that shot out from beneath the leaves. It was all much tougher. But still I hate to pick 'em.

It goes back I suppose to a spring morning, cold, before the sun up, early dew wet through the tennis shoes, standing at the corner for the bus and skinny sister looking anxiously into your eyes.

"Where's the lunch?"

"I forgot."

The sudden look of desperation, thoughts visibly crashing through the thin girl's head, she, measuring the time to run home and retrieve the forgotten brown paper bag, maybe missing the bus and the whole day. "What'da you do that for?" She hands the small boy her sweater. "Wait." But even as she darts into the road, the yellow and black onetime school bus turns the corner. Too late. The girl moves one direction away, then back toward the boy, uncertain and then as if time itself had made up her mind, she comes back to the corner and propels the boy toward where the bus stands open door, waiting.

"Eckersly's?" the lady at the wheel calls out. "You kids waiting for Eckersly's?"

The thin-faced girl nods and pushes again at her brother's narrow shoulders and the two of them stumble up the bus steps. It is quiet on the bus and the others can hear them when they begin to talk about the forgotten lunch bag.

"You think I can remember everything?" The girl's voice is tense, trying to be angry. "What are we going to eat?"

"Strawberries. I like strawberries anyway."

"Strawberries alone isn't enough. They make you sick if you don't eat something else with them," she says.

"And water. They got water, ain't they?"

The girl stops scolding and the two of them ride close together, the warmth of their thighs against one another in the cold, jostling bus that smells sour from the sweat of yesterday's pickers and is heavy with the exhaust fumes that seem to come up through the worn floor. When the bus finally rocks into the dirt tracks leading off the road and into the field, they watch out the window at the expanse of green berry bushes and wait while the driver threads the bus along the two narrow ruts into the field to the picking station.

"Just stay near me and don't say anything," the girl says.

"You are too little to pick. They don't like little kids like you here. You don't pick enough." The boy follows her down the bus steps and up to the weigh station.

"He picking?"

"He's my brother. I gotta look after him," the girl says. "He's gonna help me."

"Why can't I pick myself?"

"What's that?" the man at the station tries to catch the words.

The boy slips a little further behind his sister. "He's gonna help me," she says again and takes a number and an empty berry flat from the pile.

"He's too young to pick" the man says. "You keep out of the way and don't mess around out there, or out you both go."

The sun grows hot in the afternoon and the girl looks up again at the boy, leaning with one hand on her back above her hip, brushing the loose strands of hair from her face. She sees the berry-stained face smiling, like a pup's looking for an ear rubbing as he comes back toward the tray with his hands cupped full of berries. They rattle into an empty hallock, barely covering the bottom. "You hungry?" she asks.

"Huh huh," the boy says. "I ate all the berries I could."

"Well. A little longer," she says and goes back to working her fingers beneath the bush that flows over her knees. She picks straddling the rows, bending constantly to pull aside the leaves and uncover the fruit.

It is late in the afternoon when she has her card punched at the weigh stand. The others are already in the bus. "You had a good day. That brother help much?" the man asks as he hands her back the card.

"Could I have a dollar today?" the girl replies.

"You quitting?" He is afraid of losing pickers, especially good ones.

"No. I just need the dollar."

"What for?"

"Lunch," she says simply.

"It's damn near dinner time. Didn't you get enough to eat in the berry patch?" The bus driver beeps the horn at them. "Here," and the man hands her a dollar bill. "That will go against your picking today," he warns and they run to the bus.

The sun is late afternoon hot and the wind blows in thick and warm through the open window as the bus begins to work toward town through the traffic. The boy shuts his eyes against the raw taste on his tongue, against the hard light of the sun and against the hot air blowing into his face and in the deep red he sees against his eye, there comes into focus strawberries, red, ripe strawberries.

Death of Trotsky

I imagine Trotsky is dead by now. When we parted last, he was quite old. His teeth had lost their menace and were yellowed and soft from the peanuts and bread.

Trotsky begged in those last years. He was sagging at the belly and there was a cunning fawning to the way he played for peanuts. In the beginning, when we were both younger, he would rise up and roll his head from side to side with imperial impatience demanding to be fed.

We knew Trotsky as the biggest bear in the world, not because he was in fact, but because he was our bear and on Saturdays, a trip to the zoo was never to see the monkeys or play on the swings or anything but to see Trotsky.

I guess it was because I was such a small boy when we met for the first time that I remember the details so, the rain-wet concrete floor to his cell littered with peanut shells, the yellow-brown water of the small pool that took up a third of the space inside the bars, the stool, not yet washed down by the keeper and tracked by his padded feet here and there in sour testimony to his restless pacing.

There was a small handrail outside that kept the spectators two or three feet from the cage so the bear would not reach them through the bars. And we would climb on that handrail and throw the peanuts toward Trotsky. Sometimes he would catch them in mid flight with what seemed a slow, certain turn of his head. When we threw badly, they would bounce off his chest and after awhile, the bear would drop to all fours and sniff the scattered nuts from the floor of his cage.

I have always had it in the back of my mind to tell you about Trotsky, not because he was a great silver gray bear in a cage, there were all kinds of bears in cages, but because he was always there. Christmas and birthdays would come, and come again, and summer days at the beach and berry picking and apples in the fall, weddings and Halloween, and all the things that mark your growing. Trotsky was always there.

Looking back I understand now the surprise I felt at seeing him there each time I went back to the zoo, in the same cage, the second from the end, with the same small, dank, concrete den in one corner, Trotsky on his haunches amidst the feces and peanut shells, looking coldly at me each time.

He had been behind bars all those years of my growing and had never been free, never with a she-bear, never wandering through the woods, his belly fat with summer harvest. Oh, they marked his birthday, the day he was captured. Now and again a reporter, usually the newest reporter on the paper, would come up with a zoo story and it would be about Trotsky getting a special treat because it was his birthday and they would write gaily of the "old boy" enjoying his passing years.

But it comes to me now that same feeling of sadness I felt each time I saw him, knowing that he would die there, regarded always like a property of the city, like a drinking fountain or the park's public toilets, something to serve the taxpayers.

In our town, now the commissioners and the mayor are arguing over who is going to pay for the upkeep of our zoo. Our flock of penguins have died, all but one, and the fat seal was taken out of the seal tank. He was sick and they cut him open and found his belly full of coins because the seal, away from the sea, mistook the coins tossed in the pool for sea shells and ate them, and died.

The zoo keeper says everything is fine in our zoo if they can only have more money. The elephants are having more baby elephants and the monkeys are like monkeys born in captivity everywhere, arguing and eating peanuts. And there are fancy new lion and tiger pits and a special water-filled tank for the polar bear and new cages that do not look like cages for the other bears.

This was supposed to be, the zoo people say, a place for the kids to visit and have a good time looking at the animals and learning things about the animals in cages and pits.

But it seems not too many people are doing that anymore and because they are not, the gate receipts at the zoo are down and if you are going to keep all those animals, the zoo people say, they need more money.

Maybe now is the time to decide to look at something else for awhile. After all, if we wanted only to learn from observing, think of what we could learn with a ticket for admission into the state prison. Not the same you say? The animals don't know any better and it wouldn't be decent to go and stare at mankind behind bars?

I see the small hazel eyes of that great bear when I try to tell myself something like that and I wonder if indeed there is a place, in the world of compassionate people, to build bear cages, to justify our zoo with a shower of peanuts in the shell come Saturday afternoon.

Going Home

It was Thomas Wolfe who discovered, "You Can't Go Home Again." Yet men try. They will suck in their bellies and try.

I know a guy who went back to his old home town in Wichita, Kansas and his house was gone. There was a tree growing outside of where the house used to be. He said when he was a kid he would climb out his bedroom window and down the tree. The tree was still there. But not the house. He never went back to Wichita again. Afraid, I suppose, someone might have cut down the tree.

So we just talk about the past, shaping it, bending the days into what they might have been and never really were. We live too much looking in the rear view mirror my friend tells me. "You have got to stop looking in the rear view mirror," he says. And he is right about so many things, this friend, that I feel guilty, catching myself from time to time glancing back.

There was a window cleaner coming down the steps of the brown frame house. You could see he was a window cleaner, he carried the pail and the chamois and the look of a curious man.

"Do you know if the Evans' family still live here?"

He shifted the ladder on his shoulder as he answered, "The old lady's upstairs. Just knock good and loud."

The front door was open ajar to the summer air and from beyond the screen her voice carried to the porch, speaking to herself or the window cleaner, it was not clear. It was about the money to pay him and she didn't hear the knocking. "Is it still the same price?"

The window man put away his tools and came back to the door and we walked inside together. At first she did not notice there were two of us.

"How much is it, the same as last time?"

"Same. But I gotta get more money for this soon. Can't keep doing things at these prices. Everything's going up." Then glancing over his shoulder by way of introduction, he added: "That her?"

"Mrs. Evans? I used to live down the street. Maybe you remember. We used to sell you crabapples about this time of year. Masons lived next door, didn't they? How are Arthur and Beth?" I was talking too fast for her. She had been kind to us then but maybe we were not that important to remember. There was that intimidation, that stepping so far back into her life and your own.

"Why, you are Georgie Pratt," she said and her eyes looked quizzically across the years at what was the snot-nosed neighbor.

It had been nearly forty years and as she spoke, I could hear, for an instant, a voice from the empty street calling "Georgie Porgie puddin' 'n pie." And there was the smell of fresh sawdust her sons carried in huge sacks to their basement for winter fuel, and though she carried a cane, there was a certain casualness of age about her. It was indeed Mrs. Evans.

"How's your mother?" she asked. "My, she was a fine woman with all you kids. Why you used to come in here and tell the most awful tales, the wildest stories."

And after that we remembered in fast succession the unimportant things like Mr. Mason's apple tree. We called him "Old Man Mason," but not to Mrs. Evans' face, she was his neighbor. And we talked about the Pappas kids from across the street and the girl with the golden hair, Gloria, who lived in the bake shop in the lane. We remembered all that.

"Your husband was a school teacher, wasn't he?"

"A school principal," she corrected. The others, the sons and the daughters were school teachers. The Evans family was always the class family in the neighborhood.

And the Pappas kids? Their old man had a stroke in the family fruit stand by the railroad depot and the boys made a rowboat out of boards to sail away from home in, and they sealed the cracks with tar they pried from the road and melted on the kitchen stove. The boat sank and their old man screamed at them from his sick bed.

"Johnny Pappas came to see me one day. He was in the Air Force," Mrs. Evans was saying. "Oh my, but I wish my son was here to see you," and she fingered the back of a chair nervously as thoughts came flooding back more quickly now of those depression days. "Yes, they were very difficult days for everyone," she said, half musingly.

We exchanged slips of paper with telephone numbers and addresses and she said that her son comes south to the United States and that he would call. It was the window cleaner who ended it. He had been watching, listening for something to be born out of the past, but it had proved quite dead. "Well, gotta go," he announced. He spoke for us all.

There was a familiar dust in the alleyway, and a house and a shed and a dirty gasoline station was still there. But there were fences where there had been none before. I think it was Einstein who believed that everything that ever has been is still there, and everything that ever will be is already here. It has something to do with time and space.

But to me? Only Mrs. Evans remains, and even she ain't the same.

As the World Turns

The restaurant is beneath the street level. It doesn't really matter about the correct address. It is enough to say it is in one of those neighborhoods where old folks live in turn-of-the century apartment blocks, in small rooms with overhead extension cords to improvise their way into the comforts of twentieth century living.

In such an apartment a man has been known to fry an egg for breakfast on an upturned flat iron and the electrical cords connecting heating pads, sun lamps, radios, and hair curlers often look like strings of crab grass across the apartment ceilings. And from these places come the mid-morning people who maneuver into the self-service restaurant.

There is a couple, stalling at the coat rack to take in the whole restaurant, casually running an eye over their favorite booth which is beneath the corner heater. Someone else is there. They walk through the restaurant gathering up an empty milk carton, a water glass. They create for themselves, at another table, the appearance of having just finished breakfast. Then they talk and wait and watch their corner booth until it comes empty.

There's a man who sells pencils outside the entrance of a nearby store. Somewhere in the half hour before the noon rush, he appears, speaking loudly to himself as he passes through the line with his pot of tea. His conversation is animated and unabashed. There is no doubt in your mind that though the seat across the table is empty, he is indeed talking to some specific person of whose presence he, and he alone, is aware.

A semi-retired night watchman joins the group most mornings, recounting to strangers how the crooks are making America unsafe for good honest citizens and in time the phrases: "Keep America free..." and "Hang a few..." and "Outlaw guns and the outlaws will have all the guns..." rise from the coffee and cigarette smoke where he sits. There's an aging theatrical agent there, too, and an old dolly who sees something in the night watchman that the years have obscured from all but the most optimistic.

So it was, not long ago, that the lady came into the restaurant, a stranger, thin with a worn fur collar on her brown cloth coat that had been cut long ago for a young woman. She wore a trace of timid lipstick and her eyes watered from the warmth of the room as if she had been out in the wind or the cold a long time. She would have gone unnoticed from the start except for the fact that she sat in the corner booth beneath the heater her first day and she was talking to herself.

She had a teapot and a cup and saucer and even after the bus boy had cleaned away the dishes and officially wiped the table clean two or three times with his wet towel, she stayed on, one hand on her half empty cup. The couple who owned the table fidgeted with their empty milk carton, tried staring hard at the lone figure and finally gave up in the rush of noon time customers. The woman was still talking to herself, not like the pencil peddler, not loud for everyone to hear, but softly, intimately, as if explaining earnestly and apologetically to someone she imagined was sharing her table.

The next day she came again, half muttering and smiling to herself, but not in time for the corner table. The couple had arrived early and established their territory. The second day the lady sat near the middle of the room. She had not noticed the corner table occupants, nor the loud, curious looks of the night watchman and his friends. Nor had she noticed the pencil pusher, until he, moving in his own world, loudly pushing chairs and scolding and exchanging argumentative remarks with himself, sat down at the table next to hers. But he saw her. For an instant you could see he was uncertain whether or not this stranger was making fun of him. Then he turned away, not caring, but keeping one eye casually on her table.

After awhile, even the night watchman stopped talking and all watched while the pencil peddler talked to himself and the little lady kept explaining things softly to her unseen companion.

"Dammit, it ought to be warmer outside. Ought to be getting warmer every day and isn't," the pencil peddler said loudly. But now his head was turned to the lady's table. She paused and looked across at him for the first time. Her watery eyes opened wide in surprise seeing the thin faced man in his red leather cap and unshaven chin staring back at her. "Birds can't hardly live in this cold. Need to feed 'em, keep 'em alive until it's warmer," said the pencil pusher.

"My name's Alyce," she said and she spoke her name as if it were spelled like that, with a "y" and all.

"It's God's work," the peddler said. "But we got to help. Can't expect people to stand around freezing. Nor birds either. Got to keep the world warm. Too many cold people." He stopped and looked angrily at the lady.

"Could I have some more tea, Edward?"

The peddler said nothing, but quickly shot a glance around the room and then picked up his teapot and poured what was left into the lady's cup. "Nobody's named Edward. Ain't no Edwards here." And he sat down and resumed talking about birds and the weather. But Alyce was listening to him and from time to time she would nod and smile and say something back. He never seemed to pay any attention to that.

They were together that afternoon in front of the store where the peddler sold his pencils and they appeared together the next day, nodding and talking more quietly now as they went through the self-service line. But they have been gone ever since, talking to one another somewhere in that world of small stale apartments, and the restaurant beneath the street level has not been quite the same.

Rose Lady

The lady grew her roses behind one of those twisted wire fences, that was no higher than a short-legged poodle, but laced in loops along the curb so that it separated the footfalls and puppy calls from the well worked soft soil of her rose bed.

She was one of the last of her kind, garden gloves, a straw hat that folded in gentle brim over her eyes, long skirts and square-heeled garden shoes. You had the feeling she was out of Buckingham Palace, maybe not one of "the family," but certainly with the manner of one born to serve in the house.

"Good morning." And she would look up expectantly, smile, and with a great yellowing rose bud in her hand, remark about the beauty of the day all the while plucking delicately at the small lower leaves of the rose stem in her hand. "That is beautiful," she would say. "A truly lovely rose."

And without another word, she would hand it to you, a gift.

It didn't matter that her caller was a five or six year old boy. It didn't matter that she knew the rose would depart immediately as a form of barter for candy, or on good days an ice cream from the old Irish lady who ran the corner confectionary. She handed it over as if she were passing it to a promised lover, a gift for a king, a last gesture to a passing friend. It was nice.

The roses began early in spring and bloomed through the summer. They took up a majestic place in her small front yard right into fall. Then, in early winter, the bushes were pruned neatly back and the rows worked and cleaned for another spring.

We never noticed the years taking her down. Life moved too swiftly for us to pause by the fallen and bent wire fence, to chase the dogs from the rows of roses, or to even notice when the thin stems grew loose and straggling from the wild stalks. But it all happened, a year at a time.

We had long since stopped calling for free roses to barter at the corner store. Occasionally, usually late in the afternoon when the summer sun had eased, she would appear again in the garden, moving confused and exasperated among the bushes where the weeds grew tall and the budding flowers spread into small, untrimmed branches.

"For your mother," she would say, brushing back the worn and soiled straw hat. The roses she gave you then were cut short in the stem, an assortment of colors, not of the same elegance they once were.

In that spring when she didn't come out at all, a relative from back East came to live with her, a young lady who left early in the morning and came back briskly in the evenings. She herself took down the small wire fence. Later she stood on the curb supervising the man who came to put in the lawn where the front yard rose garden grew.

They pulled the roses out by the roots, shaking the loose sod from the naked, clinging strands that seemed to reach out for the earth.

"Whatcha going to do with those?"

The gardener didn't answer, but continued to toss the bushes onto a pile.

"If you don't want them, can I take them home?"

"They ain't no good. Too old," he said. "Take 'em if you want."

And carefully, handling the pointed thorns between our fingers, we carried them home and dug them in along the back fence. They are there now, tall and glamorous in the sunshine, deep reds and yellows that come back with vigor with the late spring. Sometimes, when they look so good, we think that maybe we should take them seriously, prune them carefully in the fall, bud them in spring and then enter them in the great Rose Festival competition.

The lady would like that for her rose bushes, and we owe her something, someday.

Cop on the Beat

It has been a long time since I last saw a policeman on the beat. Oh, there are the special cops in turn-of-the-century Bobbie hats marching through Old Town as part of the tourist attraction, and television movies like the Blue Knight imply they still walk the beat in places like Los Angeles and New York City.

But I'm talking about cops like Old Jack Marshal who used to walk around Second and Third and Yew Streets and tour the park in the evenings. He would stop outside of Bab's Drugstore and with a heavy brass key, open the blue box hung on the telephone pole, reach inside, take the telephone off the hook and "call in." It only took a second. You could never hear what it was he said, even standing close. And he would slam the box shut, turn the key, and turn again, ready for action.

"What are you kids up to?" The question was of the nature of asking, "What's new?" Friendly. And he would add, "Where's Ernie Turner today? Or Hughie Forbes and that Ferguson kid I had to talk to last week?"

Most of the time Marshal wouldn't wait for an answer. He would just rattle off a few names to let you know you were all on his mind, and then walk away toward the beach. You didn't have to see him to know he was there. The whole park and the beach were his beat and with that quiet way he had of coming up on you from out of nowhere, you had to figure he was with you no matter what you were doing. So most of the time you didn't do much, or if you did, you did it fast.

Smokin' was something he didn't like. When he came across you smokin', he would lose the friendly look in his face and tell you get on out of the park or make some other nasty crack that let you know there wasn't much going for you with him at that time.

After awhile they took him off the beat and put him in a patrol car, but he cruised around the neighborhood a lot for awhile. And much later when I was a police reporter, I knew him as a plain clothes detective and a good one doing murder cases and robberies. He was as close to a Jack Webb detective as you will find in real cop shop, a homicide and robbery man, and moving up in the force.

They said he got in trouble once handling a rough customer in the lobby of the city jail. They say he bounced the rough character up and down on the marble floor in front of everybody and the only guy who didn't come forward to blow the whistle on him was the blind man who ran the cigar counter.

Now they probably had as much going on in the crime business in those days as we do today, what with people being so poor and all during the depression. Guys like George Dupree ended up robbing grocery stores and not because it was easier than working, but because there was no workin' to be had.

But I can remember leaving bicycles unlocked and leaning against a fence at the beach for a whole day. Nobody every heard of a purse snatching or a mugging, and except for Esther Ludlow, who used to complain to Marshal that the ''boys were after her,'' and she was right, there wasn't any trouble with sex fiends or ex-hibitionists while Marshal was around.

Looking back, you have to believe he was part of our environmental training in those days. But now? Now we are all up-tight about air pollution and disposable cans and saving old buildings as mementos of our past and the kids are learning these values well. What's missing among the good things we could save is a cop on the beat for people to live with. A good cop, like Jack

Marshal, is part of the environment too. And that has a lot to do with the quality of life, believe me.

Landlording

A friend has sent me a book called, "How to Make a Solid Profit in the Apartment Business." It comes with all the secrets.

"How to Look for a Building; How much to Pay (Save Thousands by Following the Author's Buying Secrets); Pets, Pools, and Pests..." Here are all the things you need to know about getting rich in the apartment business, except what to do when someone doesn't pay the rent.

Now people are doing it today who never ever thought about becoming landlords. The whole thing is taking off and this friend who sent the book says I ought to get in on it too, and asks, as the book cover asks—"Seeking an exciting second career? Or simply a sound investment that will be a foolproof hedge against inflation...?"

Even as I wet my lips in anticipation of the profits, there comes to mind the image of old man McConachie. He was a landlord by birth and grew into the bowler hat like most of us grow into our second molars. He stood six feet or more with a heavy roundness that began about his shoulders and stayed with him all the way down his frame to his knees. He wore large, high bottom black boots that thundered on the front steps like a Napoleonic cannon.

Our rent was thirty dollars a month, more than we should have been paying on "Mother's Allowance," as the dole was then called. But Momma was an "uppity" lady in her way and even in those days she wanted to bring her kids up in a decent neighborhood.

On the first of each month, two of us would escort the thirty dollars in cash to McConachie's house and wait for his handwritten receipt—"$30. Paid. March, 1937. E.P. McConachie." It was all recorded in thick dull pencil on a lined sheet from the pad he carried in his vest pocket. He would lick his thick thumb and pull the sheet from the small wire pad and hand it across without a word.

The idea was always to get to McConachie's house with the rent before he came around looking for it. With ten kids rattling around his rental, he was an agent for the owner, you were never too confident in what condition he would find the place.

It was two days past the first of the month when we heard him coming up the front steps. We waited for him to twist the broken doorbell that sounded like the winding of a clock when you turned the handle.

"Mr. McConachie," Momma shouted with surprise and pleasure, thrusting the thirty dollars into his hand. Her allowance check had arrived that day and the cash was fresh from Patch's Grocery. He lifted his bowler and began to peer in the front door, turning his small head on his thick shoulders.

I was dancing at Momma's knees and excited with the fact we had a caller. "Come on in and see what my brothers have done in the basement," I hollered. Momma blanched and the big man looked down at me.

"It's nothing," she said and stepped outside on the porch trying to pull the door shut in my face.

"They built a nine hole golf course," I hollered.

"A what?" McConachie said.

"Get inside before you get cold," Momma said pushing me toward the house.

"All around the woodpiles," I was hollering, trying to impress him with the fact the boys had worked hard to chop holes in the concrete basement floor for their putting course. It was the most magnificent accomplishment of the winter.

McConachie began to show concern and interest. "How did they do that?" he asked Momma. But before he could finish, Momma was mentioning to him that we still had the pots standing in the upstairs bedroom where the roof leaked and wondered if he was going to have someone out to look at the furnace like he had promised a month ago.

It was a standoff. By the time Momma had foot-pushed me out of sight the old landlord was settling for the thirty dollars and with a tip of his hat he said he would tend to all those matters "as soon as we can get to them, Mam."

McConachie died before they discovered the golf course chopped in the basement floor. Still, I can't erase the image of him from between the pages of this book on "How to Make a Solid Profit in Apartments." It's not a role for the faint of heart, being a landlord, you know.

Santa Claus

I met Santa once, the real McCoy. God knows where they got him, but this was him. He even smelled real, like reindeer moss and leather and he had those pale gray eyes that looked right back through the entire year when he asked, "Have you been a good boy?"

I thought of him today because I read where in New York City they are having hassles on the streetcorners between competing Santas for the nickels and dimes shoppers drop in those Christmas kettles.

I thought of him the other night, too, at a dinner where Santa popped in, a Santa with an Italian accent and a black mustache. And I think of that real Santa every time I see one of the phonies on television selling diamonds and perfume and new cars. It is like they are forging checks on that original I met once a way back.

First time I ever laid eyes on the real one, I knew it was all true, there was indeed a little old guy from the Pole and he was doing all the things they said, riding on rooftops and sliding down chimneys and checking up on boys and girls, mostly when he wasn't making toys and snoozing between Christmases.

It was on the fifth floor of Spencer's Department Store right where the Christmas train wound away from the toy department.

He was sitting on a large green throne Spencer's had put there for him and there were four or five kids dodging the question in his eye by ducking behind their mothers' skirts.

"You, you there. Come on up here and say hello to Santa," and he beckoned for me to come forward. His suit was a deep, deep crimson red, velvety and soft and his whiskers were silky smooth and brushed carefully over his chest. He had pulled his cap off his head and it lay on the arm of the chair but his thick white hair, parted in the middle, seemed to crown him with all the splendor of his realm.

If he stood up, he would have been maybe five feet tall, not an inch more and when he pulled me onto his lap, it was a struggle to get settled because his round belly took up all the room there.

Close, looking into the wrinkles around his eyes, close enough to see the white hairs growing out of his ears, smelling the candy cane on his breath as he leaned to whisper in my ear, that close, I knew.

"What do you want for Christmas? Eh?"

Oh, great moments. My mind went completely blank. Bicycles, trains, toy cars, things for Momma, all the dreams gathered and harbored for that moment were gone.

"I dunno."

"You don't know?" And he laughed a modest "ho ho" and looked out at the watching faces of the adults for confirmation.

"Here's someone who doesn't know what he wants for Christmas. You been good to your mother? Do all your chores?"

The intimidation of being that close to the real thing left me mute and I nodded a positive confirmation that would have to do for an answer.

"Well, you be a good boy. Get to bed early and do as Mother says and Santa will be around your house on Christmas. All right?"

Another stunned nod and he slipped me to the floor.

And he came that year with socks and books and a football and perfume for my sisters and bath salts for Momma and shaving cream for my brothers and I sat deep in the wrapping paper beneath the tree picturing him in my mind's eye dancing around our living room and slipping, somehow, up that tiny chimney to the roof.

He was not there in Spencer's the next year. That was the year when it all came apart, the magic of Christmas, when the taunts of the schoolyard went, "He still believes in Santa Claus," changed to where I joined the others who said: "Anybody who believes in Santa Claus is crazy. That's kid stuff." From the day I saw the new Spencer's Santa Claus, I made it a point to scoff and put him down. I even had trouble pretending for my own kids when they were little, always qualifying the Santa Claus stories with an explanation of the spirit of Christmas.

But deep in the backroads of my memory, he is there yet, that one, that true Santa with the gray eyes and the magic in his beard. I know he's out there somewhere in that jungle of Christmas impostors.

Spring Has Sprung

Spring, they say, has sprung. You old timers out there may be aware whether or not it's true, what they say about spring. I mean, you remember things like Shrove Tuesday and hot cross buns, and hats with ribbons on them for little girls and church on Sunshine Sundays. These were your signs of spring. Yep. Now, you get the Pope on living color television, right from Rome, for an hour in your living room, Easter Sunday morning, if you can afford to miss the National Basketball Association playoff games. But even the Papal Paul, who draws a hundred thousand Brownies and Liecas and Nikons to St. Peter's Square for the performance from the balcony, even the Pope cannot bring Easter like an Easter Sunday in old St. Mark's on the hill.

On Easter Sunday, they would peel the purple drapes off the statues of Mary and Jesus; the choir, with hair slickum on the men and lipstick and tight corsets on the ladies made Easter the truly great day it was.

Easter Sunday, a ham and sweet potatoes day, brought a small bowl of crocus blossoms in water to the middle of the table. With the coming of spring spelled out like that, a boy felt the first tight squeeze that summer brought to the toes of his boots. The malady that could be cured only by a summer long stint of bare feet in the dust. With an Easter like that, you could be certain of finding the neighbor kids, the shinny players and the corner kick-the-canners, turning up at the gravel pit and playing pick up baseball until dinner. And it would only be a week or so until they started showing up after dinner and playing until you couldn't see the ball, because it was spring.

Spring used to do all kinds of strange, mysterious things to small boys. Sending them shimmying up trees to sit alone amongst the awakening branches, quietly watching people walk past below. Spring would send rocks skipping across flat puddles of rain. It dried up the winter's running noses and Momma said it made the windows look dirty. Spring meant wrestling on the still damp grass and lying there hot and breathing hard on the fresh broken green. It felt so alive beneath your back until the chill touched your shoulders and you remembered what you had been told about the dangers of lying on the damp grass. But it felt so good it seemed worth the chance.

Yes sir, there was never much doubt about spring. Oh, you didn't have it announced to you like it is now; I mean there was none of the flood of commercial mailings from automobile dealers announcing special rates on their spring tune ups. We had none of the big spring clothing sales or the spring holiday tour ads to tell us it was spring.

Spring wasn't a signal in our corner stores to pull out all the winter goods. We didn't get hit with television commercials to buy garden tractors, but somebody would spade the backyard for Momma. Spring was too early to plant, but it was time to turn the heavy winter soil to the early sun to sweeten.

That was spring, a marble "pie," scratched in the schoolyard dirt, and knuckles down (bonies tight) to the shooter. Then you knew it was spring.

Oh, there are blossoms on my plum tree now and my son, who was "broko lobo," as he puts it, cut the lawn the other day. I can smell the fresh grass cuttings on the compost and the blueberry patch out back is blushing with the yellow sap that brings leaves and berries later. So I suppose it is indeed spring. But there is snow on the mountains, and my hands are cold and there is a stiffness in my knees that was winter bred and refuses to go now. And I wonder, as I watch it coming again and waiting again for that flush of excitement spring brings to the young, if spring will ever come again to me.

First Date

Your first date does not necessarily have to come in summer season, but chances are it does. School's out then. You have that summer job cash in your pocket and the girl in your eye isn't constantly getting lost in the human mass of junior high school. Besides, if you handle it right in summer, there isn't the exposure to neighborhood razzing like there is if you start off walking a girl home from school.

That first date. Cammie Moffat. She was thirteen, maybe fourteen. Girls were less mature then, but bumpy in places so you knew they were different say from Alvin Conner or Donald McKay. Cammie quit wrestling a couple of years earlier and that summer had dropped out of streetcorner kick-the-can and she failed to make practice as our substitute third baseman.

You could see the changes taking place in her, lipstick and neat pleated skirts that swished around the knees. And she was suddenly indifferent, man she was indifferent. But once in a while she would give you that slow, lips together, "I'm-really-the-same-person" smile. That's what got you thinking about the date.

"Say, how about a movie?" Naw, she might say no. "Hi. I'm going out for a hamburger tonight. Might take in a show. Wanna come along?" You heard that somewhere in a Saturday matinee.

She would think you were crazy if you started talking like that. Telephone. Call her on the telephone and invite her to go out. So you call, she answers and you hang up. How about getting somebody else to ask her? Your mind runs through the possible intermediaries and the idea dies.

That was thirty-five years ago and you have completely blanked out the actual confrontation—how you conveyed the message. There remains only vague memories of your hair, water-slicked to your skull, the nervous counting and recounting of the coins in your pocket, two bits each for the show, fifteen cents each for hamburgers, a dime each for Cokes. There was eight cents change for gum or in case something came up. Better count it again. Then finally that evening, right after dinner to her house. She lived four doors down the street.

Cammie had been out to a movie once with Ernie Turner and Ernie was pretty fast with girls. Still, she was sure dolled up.

It's hard to say how she felt, but neither of us spoke more than two words all the way up the hill to the Kitsilano, me counting the change in my pocket by running the coins through my fingers as we stood in line for tickets. Cammie had picked a summer dandelion and she stood blowing away the puff as if deciding something very secret with each puff. I hoped it was about me.

I can't tell you the name of the movie, couldn't have told you that night either. Everything was concentrated on the decision of when and how to put my arm around the back of her seat. Just lean back and be casual. Oops, she moved. Try stretching and let your arm fall accidentally over her shoulder. Why not just settle for holding hands? Her hand is right there on the arm of the seat. Somewhere in that double feature we got to hold hands; I think it happened accidentally when I went to move her coat.

The hamburger and the walk home were like it was in the movies, waiting, expecting, planning and nothing happening. Then, at the door—"Well, it sure was nice."

"Yes."

Silence.

"Guess we better say goodnight, eh?"

"I guess."

Silence.

"Well, goodnight."

"Goodnight."

Silence.

We would have been there until fall if her mother had not opened the front door. "Cammie. That you? It's past ten o'clock, dear."

"Yes, Mother."

"Well, goodnight."

"Goodnight." And the whole dialogue started over again until finally you stumbled down the stairs and headed off whistling to the night as if you were walking on three feet of air. The last glimpse you had of Cammie was as she turned on that slow smile that seemed to say: "I-am-really-the-same-person." And how the hell can you kiss a third baseman on your first date?

Word got around in a hurry. Ernie Turner had spread a story in the neighborhood like we had eloped. You would think we had been caught in a three dollar motel by Father Flannigan the way they all handled my Cammie Moffat romance. It got so bad we never went out again and I had all but removed it from memory until the little guy up the street went out on his first date last week. His mother told me.

"Whadya know. Our Charlie's got a girl," she said. Then his old man told me. "Yea. Charlie went on his first date." And there was something of the "ain't he cute" mischief in their spreading the news that brought back the memories of Cammie Moffat.

I guess kids don't stand on the porch scuffing the polish off the toes of their shoes like they used to while trying to decide whether to kiss her on the cheek or on the lips or to run. But the struggle must be the same. It's got to be one of the toughest days in a man's life, even for Charlie.

Teenage Crush

I have not seen the girl in more than thirty years, and yet I have seen her often in the reminiscence of that teenage crush that somehow haunts you into middle-age.

She was short and dark haired with large timid eyes and her old man recognized the rogue in me: "You don't fit around here," he said. At least that is how I recall him saying it. It may have been more gentle, but the meaning was never in doubt. I remember tentatively asking, "Why?" afraid he might really tell me. And he said that other boys who came to his house were relaxed, made themselves at home.

"If one of the others wants a Coke," he said, "he opens the refrigerator and takes one, like one of the family...." The implication was that you had to be at ease if you were decent. It wasn't necessary to tell him that in our house, if we did have a refrigerator and we did open it at will, we wouldn't find a Coke and chances are we would end up with a broken arm.

But she was his daughter and I can understand more readily now his skepticism over the punk that drifted in from God knows where, wearing a pair of oversized mattress pressed suit pants (we put 'em under the mattress for a crease and ended up with spring circles imprinted in the legs instead) who wasn't in school and was shifty enough to keep away from the Coca Cola.

Some claim our real guardian angels come to us, at such times as that day, disguised so that while someone appears sent to destroy us, that person is really there to teach us something. It is only after the years that you can look back and appreciate the lesson.

That was a hot summer day that her old man sent me walking down the shoulder of the dirt road.

It was the year of the first torpedo Buicks and they had a red one, the two-door model, with small portholes in the engine cowling. I could hear the car coming up the road behind me. The girl was beside the open window on the passenger side. Her mother was driving. They had come to give me a lift to the bus stop. But the whole scene boils away in anger, self pity and the heat and I said something about wanting to walk and they turned the Buick around and drove back to the house.

That scenario in one form or another pushed me into all kinds of things through the years. Oh, it was never the ''I'll show 'em'' kind of thing the novelists create for a man's a-growing. But it was there in the tolerance with which I met every young man who came calling to my house in later years, some with beer on their breath, some out of work and looking as if they intended to remain that way. And it was there, tilting precariously on my shoulder for anyone who threatened a rejection of me or mine. In time, it became a part of what I was as a man.

Some of that self pity an old friend finally chipped away from my hide in the mellowing years. Some of it took its proper perspective in the real disappointments of life, the terrible blows the years deal to us all. Eventually it vanished with imaginary role playing: ''What if I were that kid's old man? How about my daughters? In those days?'' And finally there came the dimly dawning realization that it may have been a one-sided love affair. Just maybe, her old man was bailing her out. That one hurts, even when you are looking back thirty years.

And then one fine day there came a face out of the past, a mutual friend. ''Say, remember my old girl?''

He said sure. ''How is she now?'' Then a telephone number

and you call, long distance.

"Hi, remember me?" And you paint a modest word picture of your thirty-year-old romance.

"Oh, sure, how are you Larry?"

"Not Larry."

"Who did you say?"

And you expand, recalling things you alone shared with her.

"Oh, it's good to hear from you. I have not seen you since college, Barry."

"No. No. This isn't Barry."

"Who did you say?"

"This is Gerry."

And you paint once again the picture of what great friends you were, of the tragedy of the teens, but it's all out of focus and finally in the confusion: "Look, maybe I have the wrong number."

But it isn't the wrong number. It's merely one of the middle-age mirages, painted over the years in that strange world our minds often visit, that world of our dreams.

"You must have," she says. "I don't remember anyone named Gerry."

Spring Love

It is springtime and daffodils are cheap enough that you see some men bring them home to their wives. Today on the freeway, I passed a yellow Model A Ford with the rumble seat open and this morning I walked to the mail box in my bare feet, because it's spring.

The dandelions would be coming on in the Fields of Abraham above Spanish Banks about now, and if we were home and young once more, on Sunday Momma would give us large brown paper bags to collect the yellow heads from the dandelion fields. She put them in a stone crock beside the stove. That was dandelion wine from the large brown bottles that cured your colds and made my brothers sing loud, and made their noses red at Christmas time.

But springtime was more, more than staring out the classroom window at the sunlight dancing over the school yard, and leaving your windbreaker somewhere so you didn't dare go home until you found it.

In springtime they took the wooden shutters down from the fish and chip stands at the beach and for a nickel you got a paper cup full of deep fried potatoes and all the vinegar and salt you could handle.

I met Joan in the springtime by the fish and chip stands at the beach. Oh, I knew her brother, but a fellow doesn't really pay any attention to a friend's sister, even if she has long handsome legs and chestnut brown hair.

We talked a while that day, just like we had always been friends and I walked with her back to the apartment where she lived. And after that came all the magical things of summer that happen when you meet someone new, and clean and lonely, too.

There were apple blossoms picked over a fence for her hair, and cherries eaten yellow and pink, and swimming in the ocean by the twenty-fourth of May because that was the Queen's birthday and Saturday night park concerts at the beach, watching some kid tap dancing to songs Gracie Fields was singing to the troops in England in the big event cool customers now call "double-u double-u two."

And in August, when the grass turned brown from the sun and the sand burned your feet at midday, we found the shade of willow trees and got to holding hands when it was quiet and we were alone.

She gave me a pin she had from school and I promised her that someday I would get one for her, too. And her brother and I, we hardly talked to each other since the spring had changed us so.

You could feel the end of summer with the chill winds that come in off the gulf, even before September and the time to go back to school. That was the year of high school and Joan was going on to high school.

The high school bus stopped outside of Bab's drugstore right down by the beach. It was only a short walk from her apartment and I saw her there in September with books, and a lunch her mother had put in a bag. Her brother was there, too, and some other guys, and they were all excited about school, the new high school. I was in a hurry I told her. I had to meet my brother because he was getting me this job at the airport where they were building a new runway for the Air Force planes and I ran away, waving at her like I was really not interested, like I had more important things to do.

Then the bus came, a big red B.C. Electric bus it was, and Joan was the last to get on. It was crowded so you could not see anyone in particular from down by the corner where I pretended to be waiting for my brother's car.

They had locked the wooden shutters on the fish and chips stands on the first of September and even the seagulls, picking through the summer debris, seemed sullen about the coming of winter and the loss of what was past.

There were other springs and other girls, but Momma didn't make the dandelion wine much after that year, and they stopped making the roadsters with rumble seats. And Joan, they say, is married with fine sons and a husband who does well in the stock market and I even seem to recall she came to my wedding. I hope somebody brought her daffodils this year because it is spring, and that can be the start of things.

Smoking

"Did you ever smoke?"

The question comes as she pulls the ashtray closer and begins to dig into her pocket for a match.

"Yes."

"Much?"

"Enough that I had to roll my own. Couldn't afford that many tailor-mades."

"Tailor-mades?"

"That's what we called 'em when you bought 'em by the pack. Ours were 'makin's,' 'roll-your-owns.'"

"Does it bother you if I smoke?"

"You mean, does it make me want to smoke again? Or does the smell bother me?"

"Yea."

"No. I kinda like the smell if they are good cigarettes. When you smell them fresh, they can be pleasant, a memory maybe. It's only when they lock up the smoke in a room for a while and you come in from the outside that it stinks, stale, you know."

"You don't ever feel you would like a cigarette again?"

She seems satisfied with your confident shake of the head. "No. If I wanted to, like you do, I would smoke."

"How did you quit?" She has the match now and the cigarette is between her lips and she speaks through the partially closed lips, pausing to see if there is something in what you have to say that may save her, an immediate solution.

"I like to think I decided to quit because I got tired of it all, the smell in my clothes got to me, the stains on my fingers. Sometimes I pretend I just had willpower and decided it was a thing to prove to myself. But people who know me better say I quit when the first Surgeon General's report came out. They tell me I was reading that story in the paper that said the Surgeon General had discovered cigarettes cause cancer. They say I was smoking a cigarette and that I just quit, right then and there."

She shakes her head, confused and skeptical, strikes the match against the paper matchbook cover and takes in the first sulfur-fed drag. The cigarette grows hot, the draft pulling the ash along the barrel and then, as her lungs ease up on the sucking, the faint wisp of burning tobacco sends up a trail of thin blue where the paper burns freely. Her lips open and she heaves a deep inward breath to the point where her lungs claim the smoke until, at last, in a relaxed explosion, the smoke comes pouring out of her nose and lips. "Cheees." She smiles. "I wish I could quit."

"Not really you don't. It is a game, you know, just like blackjack or bingo or any other gamble where you play, willing to lose or win. But you have accepted winning or losing or you wouldn't smoke."

That brings a puzzled look to her face. She taps the cigarette several times against the ashtray.

"I met a woman once, about fifty. She smoked two packs a day, every day. She told everyone in the office she had made her deal. 'Heck,' she used to say, 'if it's not one thing, it's another. If I get lung cancer or heart failure, I at least enjoyed getting there.' She was willing to pay the price if she lost. Then a doctor told her she had developed cancer in the throat and lungs and that she was dying with only a short time to live."

The burning cigarette lay idle in the ashtray.

"I remember the doctor told that lady: 'There's nothing we can do, except make it as easy as possible.' You know what she did? She quit smoking. The doctor told her not to. He told her it was too late for anything like that. He said: 'If it gives you pleasure for the short time you have left, don't quit.' "

"She refused to smoke anyway. She had a hard time explaining why. Said she didn't like smoking any more, she was going to quit anyway. But as the days dwindled, she refused again and again a last couple of cigarettes. 'Just in case,' she began saying in the end. 'It might help. It might reverse itself.' She was trying to change her bargain, right up until the end."

The cigarette in the ashtray had almost burned itself out. "Did she die?"

"Yes. She never smoked another cigarette from the day she was told she had inoperable cancer. The only thing is, when you make your deal, don't change your mind after it's too late to change."

She pushed her coffee cup back toward the middle of the table and stood up to go. "Maybe," she said, "before it gets that far with me, I'll quit too, Dad."

Hope

"Mr. Pratt."

You look up from the dog-eared *Sports Illustrated*. One of the other waiting patients glances with irritation at his watch. The girl is standing in the opening that leads to the corridor beyond the reception room.

"This way, please." She's a post-high-school-aged girl, thin with the long, clean hair of the early seventies, and for an instant, vaguely familiar. She has your yellow card and after a quick review of the statistics, she pins it to the folding wooden door of one of the telephone-size cubicles in the corridor.

"In here, please. Strip to the waist." She unfolds the door behind you leaving you in the quiet and dimly lit changing booth. It is good to be shut off from the others. There is an institutionalizing that takes over in big medical centers like this. Urine in a bottle. "We like a mid-flow specimen, please," as if you were a horse being tested for stimulants. Then blood. "Clench your fist, please." Snap. The rubber band pops off your bicep and the thick, dark blood begins pumping into what seems a quart size test tube. Meanwhile the technician offers to fetch coffee for another patient.

Now in the x-ray wing it's quiet and you think a moment about the thin face, the familiar face. You worry a minute whether you should leave your cuff links in your shirt on the peg. They are important to you. Then you pick up the magazine you carried in from the waiting room.

The door opens quickly. It hasn't been more than a minute. She must have been waiting outside for you to strip. "Chest x-ray, is that right?" She's making conversation. The slip says it's a chest x-ray.

"Suppose so," you reply and then make a joking remark about the chilly x-ray plate on the wall.

"Take a deep breath. Hold it." There is a whirring sound, a deceleration of a spinning somewhere at the other end of the photographic shooting gallery and the heavy closing and opening of some kind of metallic container. "Once more. A deep breath. Hold it." And the noises repeat until the young girl appears again. She looks at you a moment without speaking.

"I have met you before," she says after a moment. "We came to your house once, to swim in your pool." The young face begins to focus in with other young faces from high school classes, summer faces, happy, good kid faces.

"I think I remember," you tell her.

"My brother was killed in an automobile accident. You came to the funeral," she says and then you remember. So much younger, surprisingly long ago. It was an automobile accident, they had all been friends, that particular generation of young people, and so many of them seemed to . . . the thought tapers off.

"Sure, I remember all you kids, only you look different. How's things these days? Married?"

"Yes."

"Things going good for you?"

"Huh, huh, sort of."

"Why do you say 'sort of' that way?"

"I watch your television program. That was a good one last week, at the penitentiary. My husband is down there."

"Ow." Before you can think of anything to say, that's all that comes out. "How long is he there for?"

"'Til 1980," she says.

"What's the charge?"

"Rape."

"You sticking with him?"

"You bet. We think he's innocent. We are working on it all the time."

"You go see him?"

"Every week. We can only go four times a month. And you were right, those visiting hours are terrible." There is some kind of hope in her telling you this and you listen, waiting for what it is she wants to ask you.

"He a good looking guy?"

"I'll say," she replies. "Really good looking." It sounds like the conversation you used to overhear when the teenagers came to talk about boys by the pool. It sounds just the same.

You have buttoned the shirt and she hands you the x-ray card. You want to say something that will help, to reach out across the years and restore the sunshine, the laughter, the innocence. "Well, I wish you luck, and I mean that. I truly wish you good luck." And you take her hand a minute remembering the penitentiary and the summers and her brother all in one. Then she turns to take another yellow card from the patient file.

Ferris Wheel Ride

She was seventeen years old at the most, the seat of her blue jeans stained and dusty and her shoes, scuffed at the toes, turned in slightly as she stood watching the huge ferris wheel move then stop, move then stop, picking up passengers as each car came abreast the loading platform.

The afternoon had flattened out in the heat as the naked sunshine reduced the appetizing smell of onions and weiners to a burnished pollution that hung over the fair. Mothers were shuffling aimlessly after the irascible children and even the recorded music from the sideshows lost all melodic enchantment so that it blended into the cacophony of tired, midday blahs.

"You wanna ride?" The wheel jockey had been eyeing the girl since noon.

She shook her head, not to say "no" emphatically but in a way that said, "Naw, not really, it's not important," but which he wisely read as, "I don't have the money."

"Make you a deal," he said.

The easy, warm curiosity in her eyes hardened.

"You can ride for nothing if you will scream."

"Scream?"

"That's right. I'll get you up near the top and you start

hollering like you are scared to death," the wheel jockey said. He had stopped the machine at an empty bucket of seats. Less than half the remainder were filled and what few customers there were were all aboard.

"Okay." The invitation appealed to the girl and she jumped into the rocking ferris wheel seat. The jockey flipped the safety bar into place, winked and slapped her on the knee.

"Good and loud now. I want everyone in the park to hear how exciting it is up there. Make it good and you can ride all day."

She nodded. The engine roared in the cradle beneath the gears and the seats began to move in the great rotation of the wheel.

The girl looked down at the grinning face of the wheel jockey as he dropped away with the foot worn grass and the empty snow cones littered among the papers and sticks of the fairgrounds. Suddenly the air blew cooler as a breeze coming up off the river caught her hair and licked it back from her face and she threw her head back and breathed deeply. The smells and the noise of the earth, even the engine of the wheel, were dropping away.

The wheel lurched and her chair rocked in its hinge. The girl heard a squeal from the seat above and smiled. Higher. She could see out over the tent tops now, beyond the river bank and upstream where the big Russian ship loaded grain and beyond that too to the bend in the river. The world changed and she felt fresh and alive looking out to the green hills, shrouded in the heat of early summer and the mountain, the magnificent mountain in snow, far to the East. The seat jerked again.

She looked down and saw the wheel jockey looking up, his hands cupped to his mouth. She waved and didn't utter a sound. For a moment it all stood still and silent there and then the seat began to drop as the wheel rotated swiftly, taking her down and then past the engine, sweeping past the wheel jockey and rising again and again and she felt her mind and soul taken up with the movement.

She was on the way down, the wheel had slowed and she saw the others beneath her stepping from their cages. She remembered the screaming. Impulsively she pulled in her breath to holler but the wheel wasn't moving now and she was a stop or two from the loading platform.

"What's the matter?" The jockey was red faced and angry. "You didn't utter a peep."

"I forgot," she said.

"Forgot? I even shook the wheel. We made a deal. You was going to holler up there and you didn't utter a sound. No deal." He snapped open the safety bar stepping aside for the girl to get out.

"I'm sorry," she said. "I really meant to."

"As far as I'm concerned you owe me sixbits. Either pay like everybody else or forget it and take off." The jockey was reloading the wheel as he spoke without looking back over his shoulder. The girl rubbed her hands nervously over her hips. She looked disappointed.

"I just forgot," she said. "It was so good up there, I forgot everything." The wheel started again and the jockey shook his head and went to the engine.

She stood there for a while watching the blue chair she had ridden in, remembering the cool touch of the sky when it had stopped rocking at the summit of the wheel. In time, she left, merging back into the noise and the smell and heat of the afternoon.

Sonata

Vladimir Horowitz is playing Beethoven sonatas. They say his technique is unique because he touches the keys in a manner that creates a pearl-like tone from the piano. And as he plays, my fingers dance majestically across the top of the table, touching every note in a pearl-like manner myself.

How many times have I strolled casually into a room of distinguished friends and unobtrusively taken the seat on the piano bench and begun softly, at first with only one hand, then picking up the music, playing with two, aah, the Moonlight Sonata. It always sounds exactly like this. Surprise. Even my best friends didn't know. A piano genius.

They say we all have such genius within us. It is only up to us to discover it, to develop it, to bring it out.

A friend speaking and teaching of the growth of life uses that analogy to make his point. You want to write? To be successful? To run faster, farther? Then you alone must do it. No one can practice the piano for you so you can play.

So, forty plus years down the pike after all the listening and dreaming, I am introduced to Goldie Pos. "Not P-o-s-s," she says firmly, "the name is P-o-s," spelling the name phonetically so you get it right. It's important with Goldie Pos that you get things right in the beginning for she is a widow, on the plus side of eighty years I would say, and she is a piano teacher.

"You can come at seven thirty on Tuesday," she says. There is a note of skepticism in her voice which you attribute to your introduction, "I want to learn the piano, to play well."

Even as you make the commitment, there is a mind's eye vision of school yard days with a clarinet in hand and an angry, frustrated bandmaster with no patience for softball practice or the call of a pick up soccer game. "Pratt!" His shout would bring your gaze away from the sunlit field beyond the wire meshed school basement window back to the crashing swing of the baton. "Keep your mind, if you have one, on the music." The clarinet died early.

But now it is autumn once more and there is that music dancing in my fingers as I drive up to the small house, ten minutes early. The fumbling notes of a beginner's piano lesson escape through the open window.

Inside there is a quiet-looking girl at the piano and Mrs. Pos is listening attentively from a straight back chair. She reminds me that I am early and indicates the seat where I am to wait. "We are playing a song this little girl wants to play for her parents on her birthday," she says and turns back to the student. "Once more, please."

And then it is my turn and I nod goodbye to the little girl hoping she will leave quickly. It is distressing because she stands at the door with her music under her arm, obviously waiting to hear the concert that is about to take place. "She is waiting for her father to pick her up," Mrs. Pos explains. "Have you ever played, at all?" she asks.

"Only at Carnegie Hall."

The humor escapes her.

"Do you read music?"

"No."

"Well, then," she says matter of factly. "Let us begin at the beginning." She produces a long cardboard chart to fit onto the piano above the keyboard showing middle "C" and all the relative notes to the left and right. The waiting child is fascinated. Would

Horowitz have ever tolerated such an audience? But Mrs. Pos is explaining the notes and that ignominious moment of absolute ignorance passes.

"You must hold your hands like this from the beginning," she says, correcting the splayed finger style I had always imagined would mark me for another Ashkenasi.

There is no quick, easy step to music with Goldie Pos. It begins on Tuesday and continues on another Tuesday and beyond. There are exercises and fundamentals and then finally a solo, the Song of the Volga Boatman, straight from the pages of the music book. While Mrs. Pos is probably the only living soul who will ever hear that performance, it didn't pass without a touch of pearl-like tones, I promise you.

The child has long tired of the scene and now waits for her father on the front porch.

This story is hard for friends to understand and I mention it only because there is so much talk now about forced retirement and the fight to let people go on working as long as they are able and choose to do so. "Piano lessons? What on earth are you doing that for?" is the most common response.

"Well, it's a form of relaxation," I lie. "I get my mind off other things for a while." But then, how do you explain to the boss that you are planning a concert tour in a few seasons?

Driving Lesson

She's sixteen years old and tucked inside her pocket wallet next to the high school identification card she keeps folded between two sheets of stiff plastic, is an official driver's learner's permit. And on Sunday, long after you had imagined all interest in such hazardous adventures had passed, someone indiscreetly suggests: "Why don't you give your daughter a driving lesson today?"

"Today?" And before you can go into a litany of all the demands on your time, you are reminded that you have promised and you have put it off and that, in fact, you're something of a bum as a father as far as doing anything for the kid that involves your time.

"It's not the time," you protest. "It's, just that..." and memories of the sessions on the company parking lot come filtering back, bumping into a barrier or two, brushing up against a lampstand. The thought alone is enough to set your hands twisting nervously in your lap.

It's on the tip of your tongue to suggest a professional driver training course, but no, they have already made this an issue of Poppa and Child.

"Well, you get dressed and we'll go. Okay?"

"I am dressed."

"Ah, well. So you are. Well, just as soon as you clean up your bedroom, I'll take you."

"It's cleaned." She smiles innocently.

There is a silence while you cast your eyes around the room at the others. Maybe a volunteer? Nobody stirs.

"Well, okay. Uh, what did I do with my keys? I can't remember where I put the keys."

She holds up the keys to the car and fixes her eyes on you. The smile begins to fade.

"Okay, okay. Uh, where's the car?" And you peer out the window on the chance that someone has ripped it off from the driveway. It's there.

"You want to start off right from the house I suppose? On the street I mean?"

She nods.

"Okay. Uh, put the key in. No. The black one. That's it. Good. Good. Say, you have gotten better, a lot better. How's that feel? Well, uh, now turn it. No. No. Let go. Release the key. When the engine starts, release the key right away." You are shouting to be heard over the roaring of the engine. "Take your foot off the gas. Good Lord, just a little gas." She doesn't hear you at first but after a moment while the driveway sounds like the pit at Indianapolis, she releases the throttle. A deep breath. Sit back. Relax.

"What's the matter? Ha. Ha. Nothing's the matter. You just scared me a little. Ha. Ha." Your mouth is dry and it's hard to talk. The first sweat snakes its way in a rivulet down your back.

"You want to try backing out I suppose? Okay. Well, uh, just put it in 'R' like that. No. No gas. Let the engine idle you back. Easy. Look out. The tree. The hydrant. The dog. Look out! There. Nothing to it, is there?" The car is crosswise in the road.

"Okay. Put it in forward. No. That's low. The next one. Right. Take your foot off the brake when you give it gas. Use the same foot for the gas as you use for the brake. No. Not both at once. Don't forget the directional signal at the corner. Get over on your side of the road. I am not shouting. You are shouting. Relax, dammit. Relax. You are driving like Al Unser." All this in a calm, easy manner while you white knuckle the door pull.

"Stop at the sign. Stop! Use the same foot for the gas and the brake. There's a car. Hold it. Hold it. Wait. Let him go. Lotsa time. Go. No wait. There's another. Go." She's getting jumpy. "Calm down."

"How's our insurance on you?" The thought comes as a small Volkswagen beeps rudely and swerves out from behind only to cut sharply in front of us. "Maybe I better take it for awhile. . . ." But she is already dipping into the freeway traffic and all conversation stops, completely for the first half mile. Finally you swallow the heavy lump out of your throat and whisper. "Just drive in a nice straight line. Freeways are easy. Don't worry about the other guys. They can pass. Damn fool. Look at that idiot go." A car beeps and shoots by you at what appears to be a hundred or more. You look at the speedometer. Twenty five. "Uh, you better speed up just a little. That's enough. That's enough. Slow down. Good gosh,slow down. Okay, okay. Keep going."

You catch the dashboard clock. You have been on the road eight minutes. It seems a lot longer. Then discreetly by picking the corners, "turn left, turn right. . . ," you have the car heading toward home.

In the driveway they are all waiting like it was the end of a transcontinental race. There is a mild cheer and laughter on their faces. "How did you do? How was the driving lesson?" And the sixteen year old hands you the keys and shrugs modestly. "I dunno. Ask Dad."

Women's Lib

There's a note fastened to the refrigerator door that details who is to feed the dog, who is to set the table, empty the dishwasher, clean the bathrooms, sweep the garage, who is to pick up the laundry and where the clean towels can be found.

There are subsequent notes and notes subsequent to the subsequent notes that pile one on top of the other: "Where's my yellow blouse?" Reply—"In the laundry or your second drawer. Check." "What did you do with my tennis racket?" Reply—"You had it last." "How do I get to school for early class Tuesday?" Reply—"Get up early and catch an early bus."

All this of course comes from the family taxi driver, laundress, housecleaner, recordkeeper and pet feeder commonly identified by hollers through the day as—"Mom!"

Now we never paid much attention to environmental protection movements until one fine autumn day when we wanted to burn leaves and discovered via a neighbor's protest that it was now against the law. Consumerism and child labor laws, all these new movements sneak up on you like that, but none came like women's lib. Up until the refrigerator notes, women's lib had always come across as some gal wanting to be a policeman or an airline pilot or a race car driver. It didn't have much to do with a domesticated, happy woman in her ripe forties. Yet here she is all of a sudden announcing from the help wanted ads, "I've got a job."

At first that sounds like she's signed up for election day poll duty or agreed to take on the neighbor kids for an afternoon. It doesn't really ring a lot of alarm bells. She's done church campaigns before.

"Uh uh," you reply, lifting your head from the newspaper just enough to indicate you heard but without taking your eye from the sports page.

"So I will be getting up early from now on. I leave before the kids go to school so breakfast will be on the table and I'll need some help from everyone."

That brings the paper down and your eyebrows rise with curious concern. "From now on?"

"In fact," she says, as if you had never interrupted, "I have worked out lists. The kids do the ironing during the week and feed the dog. You can help by picking up your own laundry and maybe unloading the dishwasher for me and taking care of some of the little things yourself."

And little by little you awaken to the fact she has indeed gotten herself a job, a full-time, every-day, non-paying job which she says may one day put her on the payroll. It is a job she says, which will train her in things she wants to learn, get her out with people where she can help things along and start doing all the things the books say today's middle-aged Momma should be doing.

What books? The question goes unanswered as the first week rolls by and you watch her in neat blouse and smart gray skirts bouncing through the kitchen while the rest of the house is arguing over towels and toothpaste. It's like having a stranger at the breakfast table. Even the kids are dumbstruck at first as she brushes past their calls for help with toast in one hand, her car keys in the other. They have never seen Mom like this and even I am having trouble remembering the crisp, efficient, fast-stepping girl of the newspaper room of twenty five or six years ago. Yet it's there, grayed some, fuller around the hips, yet the style is the same.

110

"Somebody run the vacuum over the rug and maybe if there's time, you can water my geraniums and gather the eggs from the chickens," she says as she swings through the kitchen toward the front door. "There's ground round patties in the refrigerator and chicken in a sealed bag..." And she's gone, almost, pausing for a second run through the house, kissing the kids, giving the old man a squeeze around the waist: "See you all tonight..."

So now I am looking through the lists on the refrigerator door and wiping the dishwater from my hands. Upstairs one kid is cleaning the bathrooms and the other is learning to make his own bed. We are alone. And from eight to five somewhere out there in the big world where people are, she is at work. And the only reassuring thing left is at the end of the list that goes, laundry, bathrooms, dog, dishes, etc...at the very end is the thing that makes it okay, women's lib and all...at the end, it says, "Luv, Mom."

Louis Latour

Ever have one of those toy ducks with a lopsided wheel? The kind that quacked as you pulled it along the sidewalk and the lopsided wheel turning would make it wobble like a duck?

Well, Louis Latour is a cat that was hit by a truck and watching Louis walk or stalk through the grass, it doesn't matter which, is like watching one of those trick ducks.

We heard the truck tire skidding that night and by the time we rushed into the street the truck had gone and there was Louis sort of smeared into the pavement and not moving. Somebody produced a shirt and we cradled the broken body into the laundry room and left Louis there very much for dead, except that one eye opened now and again.

In the morning the veterinarian said the hip had been smashed and there was no ball and socket left. He said that if we left Louis alone he would learn to live with it, and he did. Louis has at least four or more lives to go. He lost two or three as a kitten when somebody dropped him off in the road and at least one or two the week he stayed hollering in the crawl space beneath our house. He came up through the wine cellar (the furnace pit where we keep a couple of bottles of Gallo) and that is where he got the classy name. So the truck accident was really just a debit to his life bank with the broken hip as a reminder.

Now I am telling you about Louis because some people are suggesting we begin a system to license cats. A writer has taken it one step further to suggest we eat cats, a suggestion offered complete with tongue-in-cheek cat recipes.

As you can imagine, a hop-a-long cat such as Louis is not much of a mouse catcher. In fact, the one time we did observe Louis working the mice scene it was a rather small mouse and we couldn't really tell whether it was a game of cat and mouse or mouse and cat.

It took place beneath a large pine tree in the front yard and Louis had obviously cornered the mouse some distance from the nearest escape hatch. Now the mouse didn't know that cat of ours was in permanent low gear, what with his crummy hip and all. So, old Louis would just lay there and let the mouse scamper a few steps away. Louis never had a chance if the mouse ever broke for the road. But Louis' tail would go up in the air or he would raise his bum hip and the mouse would faint dead away.

The game lasted most of the afternoon with Louis obviously puzzled about what in heck he was going to do with the mouse as the game became tiring. In the end, I though he had polished off the mouse and left him for dead. The cat came striding magnificently toward the porch like some Herculean cheetah with the gout and there was the soft brown mouse stretched out on the sawdust. It was really a moment of image building for Louis that lasted only a moment because the mouse, with what appeared to be a very weary stretching, rose up in the sawdust, watched Louis' retreating rump and came on across the driveway after the cat. But for the audience of humans on the porch loudly applauding the cat, I am certain that audacious mouse would be with us today. But the crowd obviously intimidated him and he turned at last and made off into the tall grass.

Since that time, we have given up on Louis as a mouser or a snake catcher. He had a snake cornered once on the patio, batting it about the head with his front paws. Eventually the snake played dead and Louis, belly to the warm concrete, watched for five minutes and then fell soundly to sleep in the best Felix comic tradition and the short brown gardener slipped quietly back to the lawn.

Now, I suppose Louis is worth a license. After all, with all the sour cottage cheese and cat food we have invested in Louis, he has got to be worth something. Then there was my wife's reasoning when it came time for vitamins and worming pills: "We have so much invested in vet fees, it would be a waste to let him kick off."

So I guess if they go through with the thing and call around asking for a license for Louis, we will pay. He's not much for back fence serenading and he's a lousy lapper as he can't stand to be picked up for more than a second or two. But you get used to cats, watching 'em, trying to outguess 'em, and I'm convinced if the shoe were on the other foot and someone was demanding a license for me, Louis would pay. He's that kind of a cat.

116

The Whale

It came upon the shore like a shadow, dark beneath the water, rising between the waves so you could see from the shore the great bulk, black and naked in the troughs between the breaking waves.

At first it looked to be a log rolling, soaked and heavy in the sea, but the glistening black sides and the fluke that reached out of the water dispelled that. It was a whale and we had never seen a whale, a real whale ever before. It was yet a hundred yards or more off the beach line, wallowing in the surf.

A thousand thoughts came trummelling through my mind, pictures of Ahab, of the Japanese whalers, the Greenpeace people whose lives are dedicated to saving the species, of the ambrosia that was once worth a man's year of wages, the teeth for scrimshaw, it was a prize, blubber and whale oil and dog meat. My God, a thing that size must be worth a fortune rendered and eaten and carved. It turned slightly toward the sea so that the tail came closer to shore.

They say they can talk, these whales. They squeak to one another and they are warm blooded and protective of one another. People who go down into the sea to listen to them detect an almost human recognition from whales. A crew photographing them recently came upon them in the ocean and approached a huge one.

They laid hands to its curious snout and stroked it like you would a pet dog.

There was very little movement now, almost as if the whale were letting the rolling surf scratch its belly against the shallow sand. And not a soul in sight. The rain had stopped and the spring wind kicked up a fine spray from the surf.

Jonah, they told me when I was a boy, was swallowed by a beast such as this. Where did they ever get such a tale? And I remember the colored photographs in the Children's Bible of the huge, open mouth whale, belly to the shore, belching Jonah onto the sand. Yes, the thought went through my head, maybe this one was delivering something. Why not?

It is hard to say how long we stared at one another, the whale casually turning north and then south with its tail toward the beach, but catching the shore out of the eyes that reflected the entire horizon from the sides of its massive body. I wanted to run, to get someone else to witness this thing in the ocean. Maybe it was dying, maybe it would wash ashore dead, like the one they dynamited in the sand down the coast to get rid of the stink. Only their dynamite sent giant slabs of blubber the size of Volkswagens soaring through the air and one hit a car. No, they wouldn't dynamite this baby. Too damn big.

Another time they found one washed ashore like this and they put a bulldozer on the beach and dug a hole and rolled the carcass into the hole and buried it in the sand like a giant daddy on a Coney Island Sunday picnic. Only they buried it, head and all, and in time it was gone.

The dog whimpered. She had dropped her stick in the sand by my feet and I thought of throwing it into the surf. I wanted to make myself known, to have the thing acknowledge that there was someone on the beach. It seemed so impersonal and casual that I angered like Ahab at its indifference. I was man and it was close to me. But then a larger wave came up toward the shore, it rolled across the entire black shape and when the wave passed on, crumbling into itself, the whale had moved further off toward deeper water. It seemed motionless, yet with each rolling break in the surf, it pulled out from the beach until there was only a faint trace of where I thought I could see it rise. Then it was gone.

The dog had tired of waiting for her stick and had run off up the beach to send the terns and gulls rising in short, evasive flights upon the beach wind.

"You were gone a long time," she said as I pulled the sweater over my head and stamped the sand from my shoes. "Find any glass balls in the surf?"

"No."

"See anyone you knew down there?"

"Not a soul," I said. "I had the beach all to myself today, and it was good that way."

Separation of
Church and State

It was easier when God worked through Father Slattery or one of the sisters from the school. God cloaked them in black suits and flowing gowns and He wrapped the faces of the sisters in tight angelic head pieces and waxed the skin of the older ones so they looked saintly clean and heaven bound. And when they spoke of what God had on his mind, you could believe they had a direct line.

"God will punish you for marking up that desk," the good sister would say, and sure enough, she would slap on two after-school detentions and five hundred lines: "I will not draw lines on my desk and mark God's property."

Or Father Slattery pulling a chair up to the kitchen table for apple pie and tea and muttering, "Ah, God will bless you, Mrs. Pratt." And in an aside to the trouble makers of the house, "God's watching you boys, never forget it. He knows everything you are up to and why hasn't He seen you at Mass for weeks?"

A fellow could handle those kind of emissaries, or even the Sunday school teacher who gave you direct messages from God on things like what Moses said on a given day or the weather in Bethlehem in late December, the Year of Our Lord.

But today every second man, woman, and child seems to have an occasional direct pipeline and God is coming from all sides, on every issue from abortion to homosexuality to school curriculums.

It didn't seem much to the world politically when Richard Nixon talked Henry Kissenger into kneeling down on the eve of his resignation for a few direct words from God. I thought at the time that Richard might have wanted to keep that conversation strictly between himself and God, but Henry was obviously the right man to have along for negotiations, Henry and God both being Jewish.

But it was apparently a new alliance for God and that particular president in the White House.

Then came President Jimmy Carter, a born-again Christian, and while he has not revealed God's reasoning behind the presidential appointments or his Panama Canal position, the President has admitted the kind of direct communication with God that was once reserved for men of the cloth.

Yet, I am having trouble adjusting to the exclusive information some people are getting from God himself, the person who can pick up the Bible and rattle off line and verse to establish exactly what God said and meant on almost any given occasion. Generally these are people who come at you with intent expressions and a question, which no matter how you answer it puts you in immediate need of their particular straight-from-God word.

"Are you a Christian?"

"Have you been saved?"

"Do you believe in God?"

The answers are never that simple unless you want to drop to your knees and accept what's waiting for you behind the intent expression and the open-ended question.

What brings it up again now is the question of abortions and whether the government should or should not help pay for abortions for welfare recipients. Nobody wants abortion and surely the Sisters and Father Slattery would be the first to denounce it. But the facts are, wealthy and middle-income families get abortions and pregnant teenagers, thirteen and fourteen, sometimes need them. And it just may be that denying the right to choose an abor-